SUGAR AND SPICE:
-A SLICE OF
LIFE

Love
Inspiration
Fantasy
Everything else

RABAB SAIYEDA ZAIDI

BLUEROSE PUBLISHERS
India | U.K.

Copyright © Rabab Saiyeda Zaidi 2024

All rights reserved by author. No part of this publication may be reproduced, stored in a retrieval system or transmitted in any form or by any means, electronic, mechanical, photocopying, recording or otherwise, without the prior permission of the author. Although every precaution has been taken to verify the accuracy of the information contained herein, the publisher assumes no responsibility for any errors or omissions. No liability is assumed for damages that may result from the use of information contained within.

BlueRose Publishers takes no responsibility for any damages, losses, or liabilities that may arise from the use or misuse of the information, products, or services provided in this publication.

For permissions requests or inquiries regarding this publication, please contact:

BLUEROSE PUBLISHERS
www.BlueRoseONE.com
info@bluerosepublishers.com
+91 8882 898 898
+4407342408967

ISBN: 978-93-6452-988-4

Cover design: Shivani
Typesetting: Sagar

First Edition: September 2024

FOR:

My Soul mate:

Boss (Hasan),

My beautiful children:

Farah and Abbas,

Fazal and Asma,

And my amazing grandchildren:

Ali and Asad,

Ahad and Samad.

The lights of my life.

Author Note

It all began when the speaker at the Seminar said: "If you were to learn tomorrow that you had only one year to live, what would you do?"

Everyone fell silent.

My answer surprised me- I would leave my job and spend time with the people I love.

And that's what I am doing.

I had been teaching for over thirty- five years. I loved my life then, when I could account for every minute; and I love my life now when I can't account for hours, let alone a minute! Every day is SOMEDAY (as in I'll do what I love SOMEDAY).

These stories are a part of my dream life.

Many of them have been written in first person because I can relate better to the antagonist if I walk in his shoes.

I hope you enjoy reading these stories as much as I enjoyed writing them.

Acknowledgment

Many thanks to:

Masooma, my sister-in-law, who inspired me to publish my stories.

Farah, my daughter, for the digital drawings of the cover page.

Shahnaz, my friend, who introduced me to BlueRose Publishers.

Sameer and team at BlueRose Publishers for helping me realize my dream.

Contents

LOVE 1
    The Charm 2
    To Chase a Dream 5
    The Carnival 8
    Travelling 11
    Now You See Me 13
    Transformation 16
    A Love Story with a Difference 20
    The Flip Side 26

INSPIRATION 33
    The House that He Built 34
    Perception 37
    Only Love 40
    A Dollar Earned 43
    The Chosen One 47
    Can You Sleep When a Storm Rages? 50
    The Shrine 53
    The Most Beautiful Person in the World 57
    Secret Superstar 61

FANTASY 63

- The Wishing Chair 64
- Wind Chimes 68
- Mittens 71
- Together 73
- Nemesis 78
- The Graveyard Shift 81
- The Recruit 85

EVERYTHING ELSE 93

- The Homecoming 94
- Making a Difference 99
- B4U 104
- The Heart of the Matter 109
- An Idea Whose Time Has Come 115
- Finally Justice 121
- Check Your Premises 124

LOVE

The Charm

The phone buzzed. True, it was the middle of the night, but as Head of Department Surgery, for Clarence, it was nothing new. As he drove to the hospital, he pondered upon his life. He had all he wanted – a dream job, name, and fame, but his heart was empty. He touched the locket Claire had given him and wondered whether she was wearing its twin that he had given her. He wondered anew where she would be at this time.

Her smile could dazzle across a crowded room. It could light up a thousand bulbs, and it could illuminate the darkest corners of his heart. They had been inseparable since seventh grade. They had shared the same dream – of becoming surgeons. The same hopes – of getting married and living happily ever after.

The day they exchanged lockets, Clarence returned home to find his mom packing.

"I'm not going to live here a day longer. "

He opened his mouth to protest when he heard a lilting laugh. His father had brought his secretary home. They both knew about the affair, and it was clear this was the last straw.

"The Greyhound leaves in an hour," said his mom.

And they were on it heading for New York. He reached into his pocket to take out his phone and tell Claire. He realized that his mom had left their phones plugged into their sockets in their erstwhile home.

"We begin a new life – no reminders of the past."

His mom got a job as a designer, and he continued his studies.

He had tried to contact Claire – but in vain. Strangely enough, her mom had taken her and also moved somewhere else. He knew that her parents were having issues, but he had had no idea it was that serious.

It had been ten years since that day. Clarence had tried tracing her but in vain. However, not a day passed when he didn't think of her.

Mom encouraged him to go out. But as a surgeon at one of New York's biggest hospitals, he worked until he was faint with exhaustion – too tired to even think. He had no time.

Today, they had a complicated case. Senator MacArthur's cancer was now threatening his vital organs. Dr. Palmetto, the famous oncologist, had been especially called from Boston.

There was a hushed silence in the Operating Theatre. Then the Senator was wheeled in. The operation lasted over six hours. Clarence was impressed by Dr. Palmetto's expertise and stamina. Finally, it was over.

"We did it!' said a cheerful voice.

Clarence looked up. It was the smile he saw first - the same dazzling smile. Oh my God – it was Claire – Dr. Claire Palmetto!! Her mom had remarried!

As they flung themselves into each other's arms, he realized it was love that had sustained them all these years, it was love that had held them in an enchanted charm –a charm that would now last forever.

To Chase a Dream

Madeline had relentlessly chased only one dream - to marry for love and live happily ever after.

All the girls at the Working Women's Hostel, where she stayed, led full, exciting lives while hers was as exciting as a pandemic lockdown. Laura's millionaire boyfriend was taking her to the Cayman Islands; Minnie's boyfriend had just bought her a gold chain; Pat was a stage actress and Madeline? Madeline remained on the fringe, never jumping into the fray

She grinned and bore it all. That is until Dumb Debbie got a date. Honestly, she was as bright as a fused bulb. Talking to her was like sinking to the bottom of the sea. Something inside her snapped.

She bought a new diary, and that's when her adventures began...

She opened her diary and began writing, 'Today Charles picked me up at 7.30 p.m. I saw his eyes light up when he saw me in the figure-hugging black dress – his gift. He took my arm, his breath warm on my cheek, and led me to his Lamborghini. We drove to the most exclusive place in town.'

Next entry was about how Charles (actually the name of Laura's boyfriend) took her to his chalet…to Sea Rock…in fact how he took her all over the place – always with descriptions of the place and cuisine(courtesy: the internet), the dresses she wore (courtesy - Vogue) and yes, the lovey – dovey exchanges (courtesy- Laura and Minnie).

Then she decided to get rid of him. So, they had a fight over a trivial issue. Exit Charles.

Now came Lester with his heavy-duty convertible. Then, Marino. Madeline was thoroughly enjoying herself. What an exciting life – even though it was all make- believe! That is until she met Stephan. It was love at first sight. He had walked straight out of her imagination into her world.

For the first time, there was someone who loved her for herself, who loved her shy, withdrawn nature.

Stephen was everything a girl could ask for – gentle, kind, considerate. They were soon engaged.

There was one week left until the wedding. Stephan came to pick her up for some last-minute shopping, and she called him up to her room.

"I'll just be a moment!"

She rushed to the washroom.

When she came out, Stephan was on his feet, pale and trembling.

"Oh! My God! Madeline! And I thought you were different!"

In his hand was her diary. Obviously, he had been reading it.

"Stephan! No! No!! It's all a lie! It's all make-believe!!"

But he had already slammed the door.

Madeleine's emotions boiled over. She knew instinctively it was useless to explain, to plead…

She sighed, picked up her diary, and began writing:

'Today is my wedding day. I can smell the flowers and hear the excited chatter of family and friends…'

She could still chase her dream…

The Carnival

You win some, and you lose some. So far, Michelle felt she had only lost. Today, as she and Steve step into the Annual Carnival's inaugural day, she sees an action replay of that fateful day ten years ago. Immediately, they are hit by the usual noise, colour, pageantry, music, laughter.

Just like the first time, ten years ago, Michelle heads straight for the merry-go-round, the same place David had dragged her to. "Mommy, merry-go-round!"

She had thought it was too dangerous for a three-year-old, but David was clutching the neck of a white horse, squealing with delight.

Today, too, the merry-go-round is filled with delighted children, with parents shouting encouragement. Steve and Michelle watch, but they don't shout – there is no David.

That day, David had dragged her to the stall where they were throwing rings - aiming at toys and games.

"David wants teddy! "

He was allowed to throw rings from a bit closer. His third ring had actually hit a teddy. With an indulgent smile, the stall owner handed David the teddy. David had again squealed in delight.

Today, the man waves. But since David is not there, they don't stop.

Next stop, the Giant Wheel. That day, a lot of people were awaiting their turn. David had leaned on the railing, clutching his teddy, with Steve and Michelle behind him. Then Steve stepped aside to get a balloon and Michelle turned to buy popcorn. When she turned back, David was not there. His teddy, however, lay near the railing.

"David!" she had shouted. "David, where are you, baby?"

There was no answer. Her shouts had turned to screams. The Carnival workers and soon the police joined them in combing the ground – but there was no sign of David.

Michelle had to be helped back home and medicated to cope. Ten years had passed – and still no David.

She comes back every year hoping to find him. She tells everyone, "David is at the Carnival. I am going there to bring him back."

Steve humours her by bringing her here every year, but she feels he doesn't know. She is convinced that the

Carnival took her baby, and the Carnival will return him to her.

Today, she stops near the railing, as usual, looking around, and her heart skips a beat! A three-year-old is leaning against it. Overcome with emotion, she rushes forward.

"David!"

Steve tries to stop her, but she picks up the bewildered child and rushes to the car.

"Michelle! Stop!"

But Michelle is beyond reason.

She hastily gets into the car, clutching her precious bundle. Lovingly, she hands him the teddy. Her hands are trembling. Her eyes are filled with tears.

"Here's your teddy, David!" she says, her voice unsteady.

"Drive, Steve. Let's go home. I have found my baby. I told you, the Carnival will return my baby to me, you didn't believe me, did you?"

She kisses the child repeatedly, hugging him to her.

"All this time, I had lost. Now I have finally won.

Let's go home."

Travelling

"Mom, look! Grandpa!" said Katie excitedly.

I looked up – indeed, the person shuffling over to my desk looked like the textbook illustration of a grandfather.

I tried to calm Katie. She was proving to be a handful. I had been permitted as a special favour to bring her along on my shift at the airport. Holiday season, crazy crowds, no babysitter.

He came to the counter.

"They will be travelling alone," he said.

I looked around but didn't see anyone.

"Who?" I asked.

"Myra and Kyra, my granddaughters."

"Where to?" I asked to buy more time.

"They are going back to their parents in California. Their parents left earlier. They are very attached to me. So they stayed a week longer."

I could still not see the girls. Perhaps they were distracted by the decorations – huge cut outs of reindeer, elephants, jaguars - there was even a chicken hatching out of its egg – the caption said, "Welcome the New Year."

The old man smiled.

"My daughter was just eighteen when she got married. Kyra is six, and Myra has just turned four."

Katie squealed in delight. She had just turned five.

The other passengers behind him were getting restless.

"Please ensure they are in good hands. They are the light of my life," he said, his eyes moistening.

"Where are the children?" I asked finally.

Before he could answer, a tall, well-built man pushed his way through.

"Dad, they've already boarded their flight," he said, hugging him awkwardly and gently leading him out of ear shot.

"I hope he has not been bothering you. I sometimes bring him with me."

"No, of course not. He seems very concerned about his granddaughters. He must love them very much."

"He doted on them. "

"Yes, I can see that."

"He has been this way ever since my sister and her two daughters were killed in an air crash a year ago."

Now You See Me

At first Maria couldn't believe her luck. A small town girl who had worked as a proofreader would now be a copywriter at an advertising agency in Boston! The next two days saw her resigning her dead-end job, winding up her affairs, packing a suitcase and bidding good-bye to her parents.

The agency had arranged for her to stay at an old, converted brownstone in the suburbs. The landlady was big and bustling, with a voice that could easily be heard across a crowded room. Maria's two-room set was on the first floor. She climbed up the stairs. The other two apartments on that floor were locked. She dumped her suitcase on the bed and went down for dinner. There were four other lodgers – all young and friendly.

For three days, she was busy getting used to the new routine. Then she began to wonder. How come she never saw the other flat mates on her floor? Then, as if on cue, she saw a young man. Tall, handsome, crew cut. He had a briefcase with the name George Larenzby printed on it. He gave her a shy smile and rushed past.

However, she never saw him at dinner – the only time the lodgers ate together. Then she said, "How come George doesn't eat with us?"

"George!" the landlady boomed. "Who's George? No one of that name lives here."

However, as she went up to her room that night, she saw him again. Again, the shy smile. Meredith and Maurice, her new friends, swore there were no lodgers on her floor. Now she was convinced there was something seriously amiss. She had heard that many of these old houses were haunted. Her colleagues at work had joked that many of these could be rented cheaply because 'there was already someone living in them'. Her blood ran cold.

That night, she surfed the net, finding out all she could about – the supernatural!! About haunted houses, visitations, ghosts! Can you actually be attracted to a ghost? She asked herself wryly.

She didn't dare ask her flat mates about George again. She was too afraid of finding out the truth.

Then she remembered reading somewhere that ghosts are supposed to be insubstantial. You cannot touch them.

So that night she bided her time. Around 11.30 p.m., as she heard him come up, she stood at the head of the stairs and put out a finger to touch him. She didn't know who was more surprised – he or she herself. Her finger didn't go through him, and she would have fallen had he not caught her in his powerful arms. Her scream had brought all the others out. They gazed at them in astonishment.

She faltered, "George! "

"George? That's Eddie, my son!" boomed the landlady.

"But the briefcase…" she stammered.

"Oh, that belongs to my boss!" smiled Eddie.

Everyone laughed. But Eddie and Maria had eyes only for each other, completely charmed.

Transformation

"Cut!" Shouted the director, and the people watching broke into spontaneous applause. Vaguely, she could hear exclamations, "Excellent shot!"

"Well done, Nicole!"

"Truly, an award-winning performance!"

"You nailed it!"

Nicole acknowledged the accolades with a smile, but as the lights dimmed, she felt her self-confidence slipping away, as usual.. As she walked to her dressing room, she was a different person from the one who had strode with aplomb on the sets. In a low cut dress, skillful makeup, scarlet lips, coiffured hair, chunky jewellery, impossible heels; she had been, every inch the femme fatale she was playing. The cigarette in the long cigarette holder was the icing on the cake. It was a different thing she did not smoke (or drink), but a role is a role!

Once in her makeup room, Clarence, her makeup man, took her hand and pressed it reassuringly.

"It's okay Nikki, I am here for you. "

He sat her down on an armchair, handed her a glass of iced lemon juice, and began removing her makeup.

As layers of the makeup came off, she was transformed into the person she really was – a shy, introverted, small town girl who had entered showbiz by accident and was now a rage.

What people did not know was that the moment she stepped on the set and the director called, "Lights! Camera! Action!" she was transformed into another person altogether – instinctively stepping into the character she was playing. Rarely did the director ask for a retake. Her co-stars were always in awe. She had no friends, however, as she was afraid of them finding out the truth about her. The truth: that she had this weird power that was switched on with the simple words "Lights! Camera! Action!" and switched off with the word "Cut!"

Nicole had a crush on Terence, her co-star in many films, but of course, she did not have the courage to even smile at him off the sets. Nicole thought he liked her too but she was too scared to find out for sure.

Of course, he had asked her out, but she had refused – one innovative excuse after another. But he never gave up. She was running out of excuses!

Her modus operandi was to let her secretary Vic, a voluble extrovert handle all the contracts and directors offering roles. Rarely did she speak to anyone directly.

Nicole's secret was safe with her as it was with Clarence, who treated her like a daughter. She would wait until the set was deserted and then she would be escorted to her car by Vic and Clarence. She was successful in avoiding all contact.

Nicole's therapist said it all began when her ambitious parents had a camcorder ready to record her every move. She could not even speak until her Dad had switched on the camcorder, and Mom shouted, "Action!"

They believed they were training her to be a natural in front of the camera—and they succeeded—but it wreaked havoc on her emotions. She was unstoppable in front of the camera and completely non-functional without it!

Nicole heard the familiar sounds of the lights being switched off, the assistants and workers completing their work and leaving. She heard silence descend on the bustling studio, she felt the welcome darkness. It was now safe to leave. With Vic and Clarence on each side, she rose to her feet. As they stepped into the darkened studio, she heard a voice.

"I need to talk to you! "

It was Terence. She froze in her tracks. She thought as usual, Vic or Clarence would come to her aid, but to her horror, they stepped aside.

Terence said, "Lights! Camera! Action!" And surprisingly, the lights came on. He looked straight at her and said, "I love you, Nikki!"

To her own surprise, she heard herself say

confidently, "I love you, too, Terence."

Then, as he caught hold of her hands, he said, "Cut!"

Then a surprising thing happened. Her confidence did not fall away. Love had intervened. As she clung to him, he whispered, "See, Nikki, love conquers all – even weird notions."

As she nodded mutely, too overwhelmed to speak, she knew she was free at last. Free of what she had always deemed to be a curse. No longer did she need an external source to turn her emotions on and off. As she hid her face on his shoulder, Vic and Clarence came out of hiding, smiling.

Terence and Nicole smiled too – who wouldn't? A miraculous transformation - a happy ending in real life!

A Love Story with a Difference

"This time, have a daughter as beautiful as you," said the family friend to my beautiful mom. It was not the first time that l had heard that remark and it was certainly not the last time either. My mom was tall, slim, and beautiful, and I, her first born was short, fat, and not exactly ugly but definitely an extraordinarily ordinary daughter of an extraordinarily beautiful mom.

My family, however, treated me like a princess. I responded in the only way l could - by being loving and caring and trying to make them proud of me in every way possible. I became a topper in school - a student who excelled in every field. The fact that my father, a high-ranking defense officer, took great pains to get my brothers and me admitted to the best school wherever he was stationed, helped.

What was the fallout? I had no friends. The more the teachers praised me, the more the girls hated me. The more my parents doted on me, the more my brother resented me. From being a naturally affectionate person, I became completely withdrawn. My heart was locked in a protective prison of indifference that I had built for myself.

After I had topped my school, won all kinds of medals, topped the university, came the acid test - marriage! Yes, an arranged marriage! I could not look beyond my parents' wishes. The matrons and movers and shakers of my mom's social circle said, "They want her to get married!" and exchanged horrified glances. They obviously thought that my parents were wildly optimistic.

Drawn by my father's social standing and my mom's charm, several reputed families (with eligible well placed bachelor sons, in tow) came to our house. After they had oohed and aahed over the impeccable decor and our famed hospitality, they got to meet me! And it was a textbook example of 'an average man sees better than he thinks,' and away went the erstwhile eager suitors (now converted to glad-to-have escaped survivors!)

What did this do to my faltering self-confidence? Almost eroded it completely. I truly began to believe that marriage was the be-all and end-all of a girl's life. My brother tried to convince my parents that since I was unlikely to marry the kind of person they wanted (I was twenty-two years old at the time), there was no reason for him to wait. He suggested that they should arrange his marriage instead. This did not help at all. I cried myself to sleep many nights, hating the fact that because of me, my parents had to undergo the humiliation of rejection again and again.

Finally, there did come a family with an eligible son. And, wonder of wonders, the match was fixed! No one was more surprised than the family friends. A well-meaning friend said to my mom, "Please let the boy see the girl," with dire foreboding. She looked in complete disbelief when my mom told her that the boy actually liked me! Finally, l was safely married (in a grand, lavish, page 3 affair), much to the relief of my family, the disbelief of society and the chagrin of families with eligible daughters.

Now came the actual battle. My husband (whom l started calling Zed) had a married sister who spent much of her time in her parents' home - as the Control Panel - controlling all the activities of the house and making life miserable for the elder brother's wife who lived there. She was zapped out of her wits when Zed announced that he was taking me with him to the place where he was posted. So, what was amiss? This was a clear infringement of the pact! The sister had wholeheartedly approved of me since an ordinary looking female like me was unlikely to win the heart of her brother. So, the wife (me!) would remain behind with the family, taking care of the mom-in-law and the household while her brother would go alone to his place of posting. She began working on her brother to change his decision, relentlessly. When she saw that he was determined, she gave me a dirty look and declared, "Women who shamelessly trail their husbands end up with a divorce."

"Not if I can help it, Madam Vamp," I said to myself, seeing her unmasked self. "I'm like asthma! When you get me, you get me for life!! "

Zed up to this time was just a pleasant stranger. The first time he actually touched my heart was when we reached his place of posting, and he saw me removing my contact lenses. My in-laws did not know that I wore glasses. He said, "Wear your glasses, you might damage your eyes." When I looked up askance, he said, "I'll tell my mom that I got your eyes tested here and you need to wear glasses from now on."

There, we used to have our meals in the same family restaurant where he had dined as a bachelor. (I did not know how to cook). But when we visited his family for the first time after marriage and his mom asked disparagingly, "So, can your wife cook?"

He looked her straight in the eye and said, "Mom, she is an amazing cook." The outcome? I learned to cook. And even though I say so myself, I am now really an amazing cook.

Then I was offered a scholarship to do research as I had topped the university. My mom-in-law said,

"Girls only go to the university to feast their eyes on boys! Shameless hussies!"

Zed told me, "Don't let her upset you. She doesn't know the value of this. Do what you think is fit."

So, with the active encouragement and support of both Zed and my parents, I completed my PhD.

Zed was always so respectful and loving to my parents that I firmly resolved never to make an angry retort when his sister (Control Panel) said something to me or his mom after a stint with Control Panel did the same. Example: Mom-in-law to me, "Aren't you ashamed of yourself, sleeping in the same room as my son?"

Truly mystified, I asked, "Where else can I sleep?"

Once again, it was Zed to the rescue, "Mom, if there's a shortage of beds, you can remove the twin bed from my room, we can manage with one bed!"

End of conversation!

He helped me to become a better version of myself. He encouraged me to take up a job, and my confidence grew by leaps and bounds. Brick by brick, the wall around my heart was demolished; and I became the kind, caring, loving person I was always meant to be. Soon, I did not care about my looks. And guess what? Neither did anyone else! They welcomed the new me into a circle of friendliness and warmth.

If I were to recount the numerous incidents of Zed's loving, caring, and sharing, it would take forever. Did we never have disagreements? We did. Did he never say an angry word to me? He did. Did he never listen to the disparaging remarks of his sister? He did. Did he always treat me with tender, loving care? He didn't. But the end result was always good. I could hear Control Panel whenever he was angry or unreasonable. I gave him time, telling myself - this too shall pass. And pass it did. Zed changed so much for the better, that a number of people who met us later asked, "Did you have a love marriage?"

So, l have just this to say, many love stories are not the Elizabethan variety 'love at first sight' or the movie variety: those that sweep you off your feet. But those that grow over a period of time. They bind you to the person you love with a thousand unbreakable, invisible threads - fashioning a love that transcends time and place, that embraces the heart, mind, body, and soul. So, what is my dearest wish - please God, if this love of mine lives a hundred years, I should live a hundred years minus one day - for l cannot visualize a life without him.

Truly a love story with a difference!

The Flip Side

"Customized breakfast coming up!" I cry as l place a plate of sunny side up eggs in front of Ron and scrambled eggs in front of Sheila.

"Wow!" They cry in unison.

I am blissfully happy. In a few weeks, Ron and l celebrate our fourteenth wedding anniversary. We have a large staff to keep our seaside villa spotlessly clean and to cater to our every whim, but l love to cook on Sundays. Our twin sons have just been selected for this exclusive residential school for boys and are happily studying there. We do miss them but remain really busy.

Sheila and l are twins but a more unlike pair of twins you could rarely see. Both of us are tall, but the similarity ends there. Slender, delicate, a peaches and cream complexion, hair like spun gold, she is the textbook illustration of a fairy princess – the spitting image of our Mom. With brown hair and tanned skin – l take after Dad. Our parents adored us and until the day of the Annual Function when we were in Grade 4, always got us identical clothes. That day, both of us had had to wear frothy white lacy dresses with pink sashes. On Sheila, the beautiful dress looked ethereal, but on me it looked grotesque.

At the end of the musical, while Sheila - radiant and beautiful, bowed before an awed audience, I slunk away.

Gran took me under her wing, and so began my true education. After Grandpa's death, Gran had single- handedly built up the tottering enterprise into the multi-million company it was now - a force to reckon with. While Sheila was busy with music, moonlight and magic, I was busy learning the intricacies of business. Dad was more laid back - not at all like Gran – the Woman of Steel, a true Master of the Game.

Sheila soon left home to follow her dreams – of making it big on Broadway. She had been brought up to believe that the world was her oyster. All she had to do was to put her hand on just about anything and lo and behold - it was hers! She truly believed in 'Vidi, veni, vici' – I came, I saw, I conquered. Mom spared no expense or opportunity to indulge her darling's whims. Dad was more practical, but then, in the face of Mom's insistence, his opinion hardly counted.

Soon, she had people swooning at her feet. Adulation and adoration notwithstanding, she was going through her third divorce. When she had married Peter Stottard – the renowned industrialist in a fairy-tale wedding, we were thrilled. But it did not last. She had left a bewildered, heart-broken Peter for her gym instructor. Then she had left him to marry Stuart Williams – the Pulitzer Prize-winning author. Again, the marriage did not last long. Dad refused to let her stay with them despite Mom's protestations. So, l invited her to stay with us. I was very busy, but l was happy that Ron was taking time off to keep her company.

I had met Ron when l was doing my MBA.

Extremely intelligent, extremely introverted, he was my mirror image. From batch mates to presentation mates to soul mates had been a seamless, effortless progression. Unlike Sheila's, our wedding had been a low-key affair. Ron was in the process of setting up his own startup and was terribly busy. Besides, crowds always made him uncomfortable. Sheila was on her second honeymoon and had not attended.

"What about your amazing cutlets?" asked Sheila with her mouth full.

"Coming up!" I say happily. I love it when my culinary efforts are appreciated. Cooking is not only a stress buster but also a way to show my love for my family.

After Gran's death, Dad had divided the company into two equal halves – between Sheila and me – and taken semi-retirement. It was left to me to manage the whole company. Sheila and Dad both are content with the handsome monthly allowance I give them, which ensures their luxury lifestyle. Ron had steadfastly refused to join my company and works hard at his now booming start up.

The only cloud on my horizon is Ron's heart problem. After many tests and specialists, he has been diagnosed with an inoperable congenital heart abnormality. The only remedy is carefully monitored lifelong medication. I, myself regulate and administer the medication, ensuring his health and my own happiness.

"Remember," Dr. Montgomery had said, "Even a single day's negligence can result in disaster."

I had tearfully promised that this would never happen.

"What's the POA (Plan of Action) for today, Slv?" asks Ron. "Trip to the beach?"

Ron did not work on Sundays.

"I have that meeting with the Chinese delegation at 3.00 p.m." I say regretfully. "You two go ahead."

I dress hurriedly and reach the office. Cheryl tells me everything is ready. I am soon up to my ears in work – sorting out the finer details with my crack team. Halfway through Cheryl informs us that the crucial meeting has to be postponed. The delegation missed their connecting flight and would reach only late tonight. Everyone is thrilled - no one likes working on a Sunday.

The meeting rescheduled for Monday, I happily drive home. I decide to pick up my swimsuit and join those two at the beach. I have given the house staff a day off and enter using my own key. I take the stairs to our bedroom. The door is shut, but I hear voices. Oh my God! I hope Ron's okay! I hope it's not the doctors! I think frantically. But what's this? I can hear Sheila's voice.

"When will you tell her?"

"I will tell her. It's just not the right time!" Ron!!

"For the first time in my life, I'm in love! Tell her NOW!"

"She is planning a big bash for our anniversary. Let her have a last whiff of happiness. I'll tell her after the party." Ron, ever conciliatory.

"I can't wait that long!" spoke a petulant Sheila.

"Don't worry, my love. I am in love for the first time in my life, too. "

What was this husky, ardent note in Ron's voice? A tone he had never used with me!

"Prove it!" Flirtatious Sheila.

I was unable to hear more.

Slowly, unseeingly, I make my way down the stairs. Now I see Sheila for who she is exactly - unlike me, she is not concerned about the family and its happiness. She is totally obsessed with herself - all she cares about is – I, me, myself. For her, the family is only a means of getting what she wants. I get into my car and drive alone to the beach. I sit on our favourite rock. The cool sea breeze soothes me but all I can see is Ron and I walking on this beach hand in hand, Ron and I sitting on this very rock and sharing our hopes and dreams, Ron and I … Take a grip over yourself, I scold myself. This is like a rival trying to take over your company - think, Sylvia, think. Gradually, Ron's image is replaced, and as the sun sets in spectacular colours of gold, orange and red I begin to form a strategy. By the time the sky turns to a deep purple, I'm all set. I drive home super-charged with my new resolve. "Hi, everyone!" I call out. "I'm home!"

"Missed you, Slv," they say.

"How about a barbecue tonight?" I am at my charming best. "Grilled fish, barbecued chicken, stewed pineapple…"

"You got it!" shouts Ron excitedly. He hastens to set up the barbecue while I marinate the meats and rush upstairs to shower and change. It's a hilarious party.

The next day, I begin to put my plan into action. Over the next few days, I employ all the tricks – insider trading, middle-men, my own money till finally I have bought out all of Sheila's shares. By the end of the month, she will be totally penniless.

Next step – Ron had named me as next of kin in his will. I call up the lawyer – no change in status.

Now, I replace Ron's crucial heart medication with simple lookalike painkillers. It would take three or four days at the most.

Ron complains of breathlessness and I spring to my feet.

"I'll call the doctor! "

"No, I'll just take my pills."

Sheila has no idea – she continues sipping her drink.

Solicitously, I hand him the painkillers. He gulps them down.

"I think I'll take the day off," he says breathlessly.

Much to Sheila's consternation, I say, "So will I."

Sheila suddenly remembers an appointment with the hairdresser and leaves.

Ron slumps tiredly in his chair. I dial the doctor.

"Dr. Montgomery!" I cry in panic. "It's Ron! "

My voice is filled with all the pain and longing that wells up in me.

"Has he been taking his medicines?"

"Yes! Yes!" I cry anguished.

"Hold on! We are on our way!"

I replace the painkillers with Ron's heart medicine. As his breathing becomes laboured, I kneel at his feet, holding his limp hand in mine and wait for the doctors to arrive.

INSPIRATION

The House that He Built

There was once a contractor. He worked for a very famous builder - and was the top man in his field. Together they had built some of the most iconic structures in the town – malls, shopping complexes, schools, restaurants, residential complexes.

One day the builder said to the contractor, "You have helped me make some of the most beautiful landmarks in town. Now I want you to make me a beautiful residence. I have bought a huge plot in one of the most exclusive areas in town and I want you to build me a residence that will truly become a landmark."

"A residence? Since when did we start building individual residences?" asked the contractor in surprise.

"This one time," answered the builder. "Get the best architects, the best material, the best furnishings - spare no expense. It must truly reflect the latest technology and the finest human creativity."

The contractor looked at him in consternation.

"It must be the safest and most durable building ever made. It is for a very special purpose, so l am entrusting this project to you. It is very close to my heart."

The contractor was even more surprised. It was not like the builder to get emotional about anything.

"I am off on my European tour," continued the builder, "and then for my annual holiday with my family. That will take time. I will see your efforts upon my return."

So, the builder left.

The contractor thought to himself, I have been working for the builder for so many years. Now is the time to view my options. I can either build him the kind of house he wants or make myself really rich.

He settled for the second option. He bought the cheapest third grade steel, glass, cement, bricks and stone he could procure and charged for the very best in the market. He did the same for the other materials required.

Soon the house was ready and was really the most beautiful structure the contractor had ever seen. Not only was it beautiful but looked strong and long lasting. Only the builder knew the truth. He knew what shoddy material had gone into its making and how hollow it was. For a moment, he felt a pang. The builder had trusted him. How could he betray his trust? Then he put down his conscience with a firm hand. What do I care, he thought, I've become rich, haven't I? When the builder returned, the contractor took him for a tour of the house. The builder was overwhelmed.

"I've never seen anything so beautiful in all my life. My friend, you have outdone yourself."

He embraced the contractor warmly.

"My dearest friend, you have worked for me for so long and so well. I have thought so many times to thank you the way you should be thanked. This, my friend, as a small token of my appreciation, is my gift to you."

And he pressed the keys of the house into the hands of the contractor.

So why is this story told?

The builder is God, the contractor is you yourself, the building materials are your immense opportunities and options, the house you build is your future. You can choose well and make the most of your opportunities or make choices like the contractor did.

So, what is the bad news?

If you don't choose well, you ruin your future.

And what is the good news?

At every step, the choice is yours.

Perception

Once, a man was walking near a construction site. Several men were hard at work hauling construction material – stones, bricks, sand and cement.

He stopped one of the men who looked particularly angry and tired.

"What are you doing?" he asked.

The man looked at him angrily.

"What do you think I am doing? Taking a moonlight stroll? I am hauling these heavy stones for construction. I am doing this back-breaking labour because I have no option. I have been sentenced to rigorous imprisonment and this is a part of my punishment. Now don't ask stupid questions and let me get on with my work."

Giving him an angry look, the man walked away and resumed his work.

Now he stopped another worker.

"What are you doing?" he asked.

The man looked at him in surprise.

"I am earning my living. This is a part of my job. I have a family to feed so I am working hard to earn money for them. It's too bad that the sun is hot, and the work is hard, but it's okay. I need to earn the money, or they'll go hungry. Now please let me get on with my work. "

Saying this, the man sighed and walked away.

Finally, he stopped another man. This one seemed calm and looked actually happy.

"What are you doing?" he asked.

The man smiled.

"You know we are building a temple for God. I am so blessed to be a part of this wonderful endeavour. Every stone I lift, every brick l carry, every step I take becomes an act of worship. I am so happy and so blessed. Can you imagine anything more fulfilling? I love what I am doing. Now if you'll excuse me, I must get on with my wonderful work. I don't want to waste a single minute."

The man gave a beautiful smile and walked away to resume his work.

So why is this story told?

The same work and the difference in attitude and approach made all the difference.

So, you can look upon your work (studies, duties, job) as a punishment and let every step and everyday be a burden.

Or you look upon it as something you have to do and let every step and every day be a compulsory and unavoidable duty.

Or you can look upon it as something wonderful that God has assigned to you – what God grants you is his gift to you. What you do with it is your gift to God.

This change in perception, approach and attitude will change your life.

Think about it.

Only Love

It was a beautiful summer afternoon. The bus was full of college students on a study tour. They were chatting excitedly while laughing, joking, and singing. Their exuberance was so infectious that all the other passengers too joined in. That is, all the other passengers except one man. Grave and unsmiling, he sat alone. He kept staring out of the window, silent and tense.

The rest of the passengers began to wonder about his reticence. Then one of the students, a gentle young girl, went and sat by him. She offered him water and just kept him company.

Grateful but still tense, the man gradually began to speak.

He explained he lived in a village close by. His parents were dead, and being shy and introverted, he had no close friends. However, he loved a beautiful young girl from the village. She could have taken her pick from the eligible young men of that place but to everyone's surprise, including his, she loved him too.

They were set to get married when his life was torn apart. He was falsely implicated in a crime and sentenced to a ten year jail term. The girl was devastated. Then he asked her never to contact him or visit him in jail as he was too ashamed. Sobbing uncontrollably, she tried to make him change his mind, argue, plead... but when she saw he was adamant, she tearfully agreed.

"So where is your fiancée now?" asked the young girl.

"That's just it. I don't know. I have no idea if she has met someone else, moved away or moved on. "

"Oh my God!" the girl said in astonishment.

By now, everyone was listening to the man's fascinating story.

"A week ago," said the man. "I wrote to her, our first contact in ten years. I told her the date of my release and the fact that the bus passes the village. I said that if she had found someone else, I would understand. But if she still loved me and could bear to live with my jail record..."

The man faltered, too overcome to speak.

The others waited silently letting him gather his thoughts and gain control over his emotions.

"There is a huge tree at the edge of the village where we used to meet," the man continued after a few minutes. "I wrote in my letter that if she still loved me, she should tie a yellow scarf on one of its branches. If I saw the scarf, I would get off the bus and go ahead into the village. If not, I would just go wherever the bus was headed for. No hard feelings."

Stunned by the man's story, no one spoke. There was complete silence in the bus.

"I don't even know whether she got the letter or not.

I don't even know whether she still lives there or not..."

Then his voice fell to a whisper, "I don't even know whether she still loves me or not. The uncertainty is killing me. My village is just a few miles from here."

As of one accord all the young people and the rest of the passengers began to look out of the window, tense and on tenterhooks.

The man, after gazing out of the window for so long, put his face in his hands, too overwhelmed to look out.

All of a sudden, there was wild cheering. The man looked up.

As the bus slowed, in the light of the setting sun, they could see the tree – it was festooned with dozens of yellow scarves!! They lit up the entire tree with such an amazing golden hue that it seemed that the sun was rising!

A Dollar Earned

There was once a rich farmer, who owned fertile lands, employed dedicated workers, enjoyed excellent returns and had an enviable lifestyle. Yet he was not happy. His son, Ricky was a complete waster – he never did a spot of work - just lay around all day, roamed around with his friends - lived the life of the idle rich. The farmer had spoken to him several times, but it had had no effect. The boy's mom had spoiled him rotten. She thought the sun rose and set on him. All he had to do was to voice a demand and Mom ensured it was immediately fulfilled.

One day the farmer had had enough. He called his son and said, "Look here, Ricky, I've had enough of your laziness. From now on you learn to work like a man."

"Me?" asked the boy in surprise. "Work? But I don't know how!"

"Well, you know how to spend, don't you? Money does not grow on trees. Have you any idea how hard one has to work to earn money?"

Ricky looked at him in consternation. Of course he had no idea how to earn money. "Well," said the farmer. "Today I want you to go out and earn some money or I am going to make sure you get nothing to eat."

The farmer instructed his servants accordingly and went out to his fields. Now Ricky was in a fix. He didn't know what to do. So, he went to his mom – his own special, dependable ATM. Immediately, his mom gave him $100.

"There you are, Rick, my son," she said fondly. "Only don't tell your father that I gave it to you."

Ricky was very pleased. He spent the day lazing around. When his father returned, he went up to him.

"Look, Dad," he said, showing him the hundred dollars, "I have earned some money."

Without looking up from what he was doing, the father said, "Go throw it into the well."

So, Ricky went and threw it into the well.

The farmer was outraged. He sprang to his feet and grabbed his son by the collar.

"How dare you lie to me! You good-for-nothing creature! You took money from your mom and tried to pass it off as your hard-earned money!" He shook him hard.

"Didn't you think I would find out? You pull something like this on me next time, I'll kick you out of the house and if you can't earn an honest living, beg in the streets. I really don't care. I've had enough of your shenanigans."

The boy was too petrified to respond. He had never seen his father so angry. He wondered how his father had found out how he had got the money.

Now he had no option.

So, the next day he rose bright and early like his Dad and went out in search of work. Not being trained for anything skilled, he was only able to get a job as a casual labourer at an adjoining farm. He came home at dusk – completely drained. He had just freshened up when his father returned. He walked up to his father and said, "Dad, this is the money I earned today."

Smiling proudly, he tried to hand him the $40 he had earned.

The father made no attempt take the money. Without looking up from what he was doing, he said as before, "Go throw it into the well."

This time the son said, "WHAT! Throw my hard earned money into the well? Are you kidding me? Do you know how hard I had to work to earn this money? I slaved all day and earned this by the sweat of my brow. How can you ask me to throw this away?"

The father rose to his feet and embraced his son warmly.

"My dearest son, that is what I have been trying to teach you – how difficult it is to earn money and how easy it is to spend it!"

The boy looked at his father in stupefaction.

"When the money came from my hard work you had no compunction about throwing it away or spending it on frivolous things. Now, when you earned it yourself, you finally know the value of money."

The boy's eyes filled with tears. He threw his arms around his father.

"Thank you for giving me a lesson for life. I love you, Dad."

The father hugged him tight.

"I love you too, my dearest son."

The Chosen One

Based on a folktale, this story has been told in many ways.

A bus full of passengers was on its way when suddenly the weather changed - dark storm clouds covered the sky. Thunder rolled deafeningly, lightning flashed menacingly, and blinding rain reduced visibility to almost zero.

The driver drove very slowly and carefully. They could see that the lightning appeared to be aiming for the bus, only to subside at the last moment.

After two or three horrible instances of being narrowly saved from lightning, the driver stopped the bus about fifty feet away from a tree and said:

"I have something important to tell you. I think we have somebody in the bus whose death is certain today. Because of that person everybody else will also get killed."

Everybody listened in horrified fascination.

"Now listen carefully to what I am saying," he continued. "I want each person to come out of bus one by one and touch that tree trunk and come back. Whosoever is destined to die will be struck by lightning and will die. However, everybody else will be saved."

Reluctantly, the passengers agreed. They had to force the first person to go and touch the tree and come back. He reluctantly got down from the bus and went and touched the tree. His heart leaped with joy when nothing happened and he was still alive.

This continued for the rest of the passengers who were all relieved when they touched the tree and nothing happened.

Now there was just one passenger left – a young lad of about ten or eleven. Everybody looked at him with accusing eyes.

"Oh please!" He begged tearfully. "Oh please, don't make me go to that tree – please, please, please…" But there was no sympathy or compassion in the others. They forced him to get down and go and touch the tree. With the fear of certain death in mind, the boy walked to the tree and touched it.

There was a huge sound of thunder and the lightning came down and hit the bus – yes the lightning hit the bus, and killed each and every passenger inside the bus.

It was because of the presence of this last passenger that, earlier, the entire bus was safe and the lightning could not strike the bus.

So why is this story told?

At times, we try to take credit for our present status, achievements, well-being – but this could very well be because of a person right next to us.

Look around you – probably someone is there near you, in the form of your parents, spouse, children, siblings, friends, who are saving you from harm. Never under estimate their importance. Never forget their contribution, their love, their concern.

Think about it.

Can You Sleep When a Storm Rages?

Once, there was a rich farmer. He had huge, fertile fields, a stable full of pure bred horses, the finest milch cows, pedigree bulls, all kinds of the very best livestock and a huge poultry farm. His huge farm lay along the coast which made it subject to the violent storms that frequently hit the coast. It meant a lot of work - securing the animal shelters and putting protective canvas on the poultry pens. Sometimes the tiles on the barn roof became loose. They had to be repaired or replaced too. As a result, he found it difficult to get help even though he offered a generous salary.

Finally, a young man volunteered. The farmer took him around the farm and explained his duties. The man listened quietly and accepted the job.

For a while, everything went smoothly. The man was a hard worker - he milked the cows, fed the animals, collected the eggs and did all his work with enthusiasm.

So far, so good.

Then one night, a violent storm hit the coast. The farmer was woken by the crashing thunder, the violent wind and the intimidating flashes of lightning. He sprang to his feet. His first thought was - Oh my God! My unprotected farm! My animals!!

He shouted, "George! Where are you, George?"

But there was no sign of George. As the thunder rumbled ominously, the lightning flashed threateningly, and the waves crashed menacingly, the farmer was panic stricken.

At last he found George fast asleep in his quarters. Angrily he woke him up.

The surprised George woke up, rubbing sleep from his eyes.

"Why, what's the matter, Boss?"

"The storm's the matter!" he said through gritted teeth.

"The storm?" the young man said mystified. "Oh! The animals! You are worried about our animals! Boss, you are not to worry. The cattle and horses have been fed, watered and penned in for the night, ditto for the poultry. The barns and silos have been secured. The protective canvas coverings have been battened into place, the roofs were repaired last week and are totally safe. Our farm is as secure as Fort Knox!"

The farmer stared at him in surprise and confusion.

"It's not my place to tell you, Boss, but precautions for calamities you know will strike are taken before hand. You don't repair a roof when it starts raining!" The farmer stared at him wordlessly.

"Extensive and complete preparations allow you to sleep when a storm rages," continued George gently. "Let me make you a cup of coffee. Let us enjoy the storm!"

So, can you sleep just before a storm strikes - exams, crucial meetings, important presentations? You can - only if you have prepared meticulously before the event.

Think about it.

The Shrine

The sun shone on a landscape washed clean by last night's rain – making it look like a painting in myriad colours. I was thrilled. I had really been looking forward to this day.

The centre stage was occupied by the Annual Fair at the shrine of Haji Waris Ali Shah, the great Sufi Saint at Deva Sharif in Barabanki, near Lucknow. Legend had it, that prayers at his shrine never went unanswered. Villagers from far and near as well as townsfolk from nearby towns thronged to it in hordes. It was always a kaleidoscope of brilliant colours, clamour and chaos - and of course faith and devotion.

The fairgrounds were in my friend Vicky's precinct - he was on duty there. Together with his contingent, he was headed for the fair. As usual, he picked me up - we made an early start. The road was crowded. As was our custom we gave a lift to some people going to the fair. My friend's deputies began talking to a young couple, Sharad and Purnima who had a small baby. Purnima – dressed in a brightly coloured purple lehenga and choli, wearing beautiful silver jewellery had her head covered with a bright red dupatta with intricate mirror work. She was very young and held her baby protectively close.

They were staunch devotees. After a five-year childless marriage; doctors and tantrics; medicines and mumbo–jumbo; they had been directed to the Deva Shrine, and sure enough, their son had been born. The ecstatic parents were on a Thanksgiving trip.

The ground soon filled up. The swings started - even the ancient contraption with maybe eight swings, supposed to represent a Carousel. The aroma of hot fried food – samosas, puris, pakoras, jalebis wafted in the air. I could smell halwa, too. There was also a stall selling chow mein. The smell was irresistible. I had eaten my breakfast, but l started feeling hungry.

While Vicky inspected the grounds, I weaved my way through the various games stalls and shops selling everything imaginable from brightly coloured lehengas, blouses with mirror work, tie-and-dye dupattas, artificial jewellery, rainbow-hued bangles and kadas; big brightly-coloured beads; pots and pans of every size and variety...I went straight to the Medical Camp. The doctor on duty was also a friend. Everything was in order; I sat with Vicky and Doc to enjoy samosas and jalebis and drink the heavily sweetened tea. Suddenly, there was a loud crash, and we rushed to the Wheel to see that one of its swings had broken loose and the small girl in it had fallen aside unhurt but the swing with a baby in it had been hurled several feet away. To my shock, I saw Sharad and Purnima there!

Amid the horrified screams, we rushed to the spot where their baby lay inert under the wrecked swing. Before the doctor or I could react, Purnima had gathered the limp form of her baby and was running to the shrine.

"Chances of survival are slim," intoned the doctor.

We followed and watched transfixed as Purnima placed her baby at the foot of the saint's grave.

"You gave him to me!" she cried. "You can't take him back! You can't take him back!"

She began to hit her head on the ground at the foot of the saint's grave in a kind of trance, repeating, "Return my baby, Shah Baba! Return my baby!"

To my astonishment, no one tried to stop her. I moved forward intending to do just that.

Suddenly, the baby let out a wail! Someone handed the infant to the doctor who examined him quickly.

"No injuries - the baby is safe!" he said in an awed voice. "Perhaps the cushions in the swing saved him," he added wonderingly.

But Purnima had gathered the baby in her arms, overcome with emotion. Tears were running down her cheeks. She placed her baby at the foot of the saint's grave and prostrated in gratitude.

"I told you Shah Baba would return my baby to me!" she cried.

As the crowd went wild in gratitude, I wondered- was the doctor right or was Purnima?

For those who believe, no explanation is necessary; for those who don't, no explanation is possible.

The Most Beautiful Person in the World

This story is based on a Russian folk tale.

It was harvesting time, and all the men and women were busy in the fields. Many women had their small children with them.

Suddenly, they heard a child crying. It was a little boy, about three or four years old. Ivan, one of the young men, picked him up.

"What's the matter, little boy? Why are you crying?"

"My mother is lost," said the little boy between sobs.

"No problem," said Ivan gently. "We'll find her for you. What's her name?"

"My mother's name is mommy," said the little boy.

"Okay," said Ivan. "Where do you live?"

"I live at home," said the little fellow.

It was obvious that the little boy knew neither his mother's name nor his address.

"Okay," said Ivan still unfazed. "Tell us what she looks like, and we'll find her for you."

The little boy stopped crying. "My mother is the most beautiful person in the whole world" he said proudly.

Everyone laughed.

"Then it shouldn't be difficult to find her," said Ivan with a smile.

He called out to the most beautiful woman in their village. Tall, slim, with blue eyes and long golden hair, she was indeed very beautiful.

"Ivan, you naughty fellow," she smiled, proud at having been chosen as the most beautiful person, "I know all my children! This is not my son! Besides, Ivan, you know all my children!"

Nevertheless, Ivan asked the little boy, "Is this your mother?"

The little boy took one look at her and burst into tears once more.

"No! No!" he cried. "I told you my mother is the most beautiful person in the whole world!"

"Stop! Stop!" said Ivan.

Then he called the most beautiful woman in the neighbouring village. Tall, slim, fair with long black hair, she was as pretty as a picture. She too laughed.

"Naughty fellow, Ivan," she said blushing. "Of course, that's not my son! You know all my children!"

Nevertheless, Ivan asked the little boy, "Is this your mother? "

The little boy again burst into tears.

"No! No!" he cried, "I told you my mother is the most beautiful person in the whole world!"

Everyone was perplexed. They didn't know what to do.

Just then a short, plump woman parted the crowd and came towards them. Her skin had been burnt dark by the sun and her brown hair was streaked with grey.

"My baby," she said tearfully. "I've been looking for you all over the place! Thank God, you are safe!"

The little boy, tears forgotten, gave a whoop of delight. He jumped from Ivan's arms and rushed to his mother who lifted him up covering his face with kisses. The little boy hugged his mother and said proudly, "See, I told you! My mother is the most beautiful person in the whole world!"

So why is this story told?

A person is not beautiful for what he or she looks like, a person is beautiful for what he or she is. The outside is like the casing, it's what inside that counts. The outer beauty may attract us initially, but it is the inner beauty, the loving and caring ways that hold us and ultimately bind us to a person.

And the eye of childhood, innocent, unaffected, unspoiled can see the qualities the mirror cannot see.

Unlike outer beauty, which is fleeting, inner beauty is forever and it is this inner beauty that binds us to a person forever.

Think about it.

Secret Superstar

Do dreams come true? No, I don't mean the dreams you see when you are fast asleep but the ones you see when you are wide awake.

Here I am at this exclusive high society club. The members are either barons or lordships. Strictly blueblood. I am at the tennis court. Lord Frederick Welmore- Sassoon is to play a practice match with Lord Thedore Fanthome - Brunswick. So, what am I, a school dropout doing here? Who do think is going to pick up the balls? I, of course!

I have been doing this ever since I can remember - ever since Grandpa brought me here. Grandpa is the only family I have. We live in the gardener's cottage in Lord Wellmore-Sassoon's vast estate.

Grandpa also measures out carefully ingredients to make his pills that help the aging gentry regain their lost vigour. When I asked him what his pills did, he answered, "They give some vitamins, some minerals, and a lot of hope."

That sentence stayed with me. What if Someone Up There is measuring out happiness and sorrow?

Surely some happiness must be for me. Then, my dreams began to gain vigour. Could I not play tennis here? Boys my age admired pop-stars and footballers. My room was plastered with pictures of tennis stars!! So, every day after the big wigs' practice and drinks - when I was all alone, I practiced for hours. I recalled everything the coach said and practiced till my arms ached and head swam.

Today, His Lordship is really in a foul mood. His sparring partner has not turned up. When he is told that he is sick, he frets and fumes, scowls, and stomps until his eyes alight on me.

"Hey, Rusty!" he growls. "Come and practice with me! You can hold a racquet, can't you?"

Oh my God!! Can't I just? Trembling, I pick up the racquet. The match starts. Can you believe it? I can actually play! We have an engaged audience. Actually, these people will watch a tennis match sitting in deserts, on rocks, under umbrellas.

No one is more surprised than I when, after a gruelling match, His Lordship comes over to shake my hand.

"Grover!" he yells, and the Club Secretary comes scurrying up. His Lordship slaps me on the back.

"Rusty will partner me for Saturday's match!"

I don't hear the gasps of astonishment – I hear only bursting crackers and see flying balloons.

Dreams do come true, don't they?

FANTASY

The Wishing Chair

"Are you sure you want to buy it?"

Kelly looked at the elderly mariner in consternation.

"Of course!"

It was a garden sale in a run-down locality Kelly had not been to before. She had found the announcement in a pamphlet under the wiper of her pick-up. She had always loved antiques and had collected a vast array of bric-a-brac. She loved the beautiful dark mahogany and the sheen of the rocking chair and snapped it up happily.

And that's how the old rocking chair came into her possession.

She put it near the window, next to her prized albums –both of music and of family photographs.

That evening, she put on an old Beatles song and lay back on her chair to allow the music to wash over her. As she rocked gently – she became drowsy and felt herself being transported... It was a bright summer day, the sun was shining, the grounds were filled with ecstatic fans, colour and pageantry, and she was dancing energetically with long haired, jeans clad teenagers. Surprised, she abruptly stopped rocking. There was a click, the music had stopped – and so had the images. As she slowly came back to her darkened room, she pondered on her flight of fancy. Wow! She said to herself – what an imagination!

She got herself a cup of coffee and switched on the lamps, flooding the room with light. She got back to her chair and rocking gently, picked up the album of family photographs dating back to Grandma Gomes. She opened her favourite photo of her mom's sixteenth birthday. As she rocked, she was transported to her mom's beautiful old house - the huge dining room full of teenagers - boys and girls in their 'party' clothes; her mom in a frothy pink and white lace dress; the balloons fluttering gaily; the table loaded with burgers, home-made pasta , mince pies, French fries – she could smell them and the flowers – just as she could hear the singing and her grandparents applauding proudly. She gasped, stopped rocking and shut the album. The images stopped.

The page to Grandpa's last photograph opened. As she began rocking again - she saw him lying back on his pillows, pale and wan, his limp hand in Grandma's warm clasp – "Never forget how much l love you…" The family, standing around him, sniffling. She gasped, stopped rocking and shut the album, utterly bewildered. She had listened to her music albums dozens of times and had flipped through her family albums scores of times, but this had never happened before. She was not into drugs or alcohol - so what this? Was it the chair? Overwhelmed by a tsunami of emotions, she had a restless night.

She took the next day off and rocking in her chair, she virtually visited her mom's graduation, her wedding. She revisited her happy childhood and relived her beautiful memories. Two days and dozens of missed calls from her office later, she knew she had to make a choice – she could either live in the safe past or face the present with all its challenges and uncertainties.

The chair was a window to unparalleled adventure, but it was the past. She knew she wouldn't be able to resist its allure. She had to do something before she was trapped in the past. So, the next morning, with the door man's help, she loaded the chair onto her pickup and drove to the site of the garden sale. To her surprise, she found the place shuttered – it had the look of a long abandoned place.

"Where is the owner?" she asked some boys playing in the overgrown, neglected yard.

"What owner? This place has been shut for years"

In the circumstances, she would have expected nothing less. She got the boys to help her place the chair on the dusty porch. If they were surprised, they never said a word.

As she drove back still bemused - she realized that some have a penchant for the dramatic and the spectacular, but she knew instinctively that she could not allow her horizon to be clouded by visions of past glory. It was the present with all its complexities on which she had to concentrate and the future with all its promise for which she had to work. She was not a prisoner of the past – she was a pioneer of the future.

Wind Chimes

They hung the strange wind chimes, as instructed, from the open window. The bones on the chimes glistened eerily in the moonless night. The lawn and the cypress grove beyond the lawn were shrouded in darkness.

It was their High School Project to raise funds for a new auditorium that started it all. Everyone had put up stalls in the school grounds. Sue sold spicy dumplings from 'Spice is Nice,' Ria had 'Ria's Rice,' Vicky had 'Virtue and Vice' where he played CDs for a fee.

Fred and Dolby had already taken a round of the packed grounds when they came to 'Juanita's Jumble Sale'. It had the most amazing collection of weird objects.

"Actually, we were clearing out the attic. Most of these belonged to my grandmother," she explained.

"You don't say!" they said in unison.

Juanita's grandmother was reputed to have practiced the 'Dark Arts'.

It was a strange collection - masks, skulls, handmade dolls, wind chimes with real bones, bongo drums, odd art work. There were few price tags. As they examined the relics, Juanita began to tell them the unique features of each object. The wind chimes intrigued Fred.

"If you hang them from an open window on a moonless night, the chimes will bring in the souls of the dear departed."

"Surely you don't believe that!" said Fred in disbelief.

"What's the matter? Scared, Fearless Fred?" she countered.

"Scared? Me? Of course not!" said Fred, handing over the five dollars. "It's a moonless night today, Dolby. Let's check it out!"

With Fred's parents out, they had the house to themselves. They took their beverages and popcorn and settled down to wait in the dark. As a gentle breeze blew, the bones of the chimes grated against each other – producing the eeriest sound they had ever heard. It was surreal. Then they saw three shadows detach themselves from the darker cypress and move across the lawn towards them. Snatches of soft, ghoulish laughter accompanied them.

"Oh my God!" cried Dolby as they sprang to their feet.

Suddenly the lights came on. Juanita and her friend, June threw off their capes!

"Not so fearless after all, are we?" they howled with laughter.

Shaken, they laughed despite themselves.

"Who's the third joker?" asked Fred.

"What third joker?" asked Juanita. "There's just the two of us!"

Mittens

I wonder whether the dead really stay dead.

Don't get me wrong. I am not flattering myself when I say I am a very rational, unimaginative person. And the nature of my job ensures l stay that way. My musings are cut short.

Another distress call. I, with my Disaster Management Team, reach the cottage at the edge of the forest in a flash. The only illumination comes from the full moon and the orange flames. The dried up hedges and plants of the once well-tended garden are ablaze, threatening the cottage itself. The fire fighters swing into action, and the fire is soon doused. All we can see in the light of the moon is the smoke spiralling up into the sky.

I can see the decorations for the much-awaited Earth Day - many inflated green balloons, the white banners and green flags proclaiming, ' Earth - our only Home' clearly. They are already in place.

Quite the conservationist, Stanley has recently moved into this cottage, which he has inherited from his grandmother. It is a beautiful old house. It stands almost isolated as the other cottages are at a distance.

It suits him as he is a loner by nature. Ryan Forest begins just as the garden of the cottage ends.

He is smiling - probably shell-shocked. I lead him inside, sympathetically. He lives alone.

I drape a blanket around him and make him sit down. I can see he has been inflating more balloons, but he seems to have stopped in a hurry. Inflated and deflated balloons lie all over the floor.

A member of my team gets him a cup of coffee.

"Finally got rid of Mittens," he says with a smile.

"Mittens?" I ask blankly.

"My grandma's cat. She refused to stay dead. Visited me every full-moon night. So, l burnt her grave. That should take care of her."

I listen without comment. Perhaps he is delusional. Loneliness does that to people. I look at my deputy for confirmation, but he is pointing completely horror struck at the entrance.

I turn my gaze to his pointing finger. There, in the dust, clearly visible in the light of the moon, are paw marks.

Together

So, this is how dreams end, I thought, as my eyes clouded over.

The household goods were arranged room-wise on white tables laid out across our immaculate lawn.

The banner above proclaimed, 'Build Your Dreams'.

The furniture, including my favourite recliner and our white and gold bed, had already been returned. However, even the curtains – the lace ones and the heavy silk ones were folded up neatly and kept in piles.

It was too early for shoppers to arrive, so I had that part of the garden to myself. I wandered over to the tables.

My eyes fell on the Dresden china dinner set and the gold and white bone-china tea set - a gift from my parents and the silver ice bucket and cutlery - a gift from Steve's parents. There was also the engraved rice-plate which Steve had got from an antique shop. He had handed it over, whispering against my cheek- "For Sugar-n-Spice and everything that's nice…" That was what he always called me. Sugar-n-Spice – his version of my name Candy, short for Candice. I saw the matching napkins that Steve and I had found after a long hunt. I felt a pang of sadness as I pictured strangers handling my beloved belongings. But there was no way I could hold on to them.

I got a whiff of my favourite perfume. But all my clothes had been packed away. Was my beautiful wedding dress among them? It had been my mother's and was very dear to me. Unbidden, an image of Steve carrying me over the threshold sprang to my mind. How beautifully the house had been decorated - flowers and fairy lights everywhere! I had truly felt I had died and gone to Heaven.

I quickly averted my gaze, only to have it fall on the mementos and souvenirs we had brought from our honeymoon in Italy. There was the Statue of the ravishing Venus de Milo, which I had insisted on buying.

"We don't need this," Steve had said, smiling down at me, "I have my very own Venus…"

Every individual piece had a price tag, and I knew would be snapped up in a trice – but how could strangers tell that every piece encompassed a story – a story close to my heart? When we were buying those things, I had thought we were building up memories for a lifetime.

The door opened - it was Steve, hanging on to his arm was Juanita, my best friend.

"Happy?" he smiled down at her.

"Of course!" she laughed her lilting laugh, a laugh I had always found fascinating. "I love the house, but I don't want anything that reminds us – especially you – of her."

"Why would I think of anyone else when you are there with me?"

She looked up at him. "I know you wanted to keep some of the sentimental stuff that she loved – but I want to re- furnish and redo the house completely."

Being the only daughter of a millionaire, she could well afford that and a lot more.

"The interior decorators and the new furniture will be here by the end of the week. So I'm going to be super busy – and you're not to look until I've done up the whole place."

Steve smiled indulgently. "Go ahead – I can hardly wait."

By this time, they had come into the garden. Of course, they didn't see me. They sat close together on the bench where Steve and I had always sat.

"For all her reputed intelligence," Juanita was saying, "She was pretty dumb - she never suspected that our threesome was actually a twosome with her as the odd one out."

Yes, Juanita was right. I had never suspected, not for a day, not for a minute. How could I – these were the two people I had loved the most in the world. With my eyes filled with stars, my heart filled with love, my soul filled with bliss – how could there have been room for doubts or misgivings?

Juanita had hosted our engagement party, she had helped me decorate our dream home, she had selected the flowers and music for our wedding, she had been my bridesmaid. I had shared all my hopes and dreams with her - until that fateful day. It was Steve's birthday, and I had wanted to surprise him with a delicious home cooked meal. I came home early, planning the menu - how many of Steve's favourite dishes could I cook before he returned. As soon as I opened the front door, I heard muffled voices. 'Oh my God' I remembered thinking, I hope it's not burglars! Should I call 911? Or maybe Steve had left the TV on... Let me handle this. Quietly, I shut the front door, opened the broom closet, and armed with a broomstick, tiptoed inside. No one was in the living-room or the dining room. Maybe in the kitchen? All clear. The sounds appeared to be coming from our bedroom. Oh my goodness! My jewellery from last night's party still lay scattered on my dressing table because I had been too tired to put it away. The door was slightly ajar. Holding my breath, I silently pushed the door a little further – and stood transfixed. Steve and Juanita were locked in an embrace, oblivious of the world! For a few seconds, I just stood there – rooted to the spot – if it hadn't been so pathetic, it would have been funny. Then, like an automaton, I silently shut the door and tiptoed out as noiselessly as I had come. I almost stumbled over a chair. Automatically, I put the broomstick back, closed the front door softly, and got into my car. All I could think of was to get away, get away – put as much distance as possible between what I had just seen and myself. Maybe when I returned, I would find this was just a nightmare, Steve would be waiting for me. I turned into the crowded interstate and had no idea where I was headed. I could neither see the heavy traffic nor hear it. All I could see in my mind, was Steve and Juanita – like a film shot, on a loop, the scene relentlessly played itself out again and again. Of course, I did not notice I was in the wrong lane, nor did I see the trailer truck. It was a head-on collision. I never stood a chance.

I was jolted back to the present. Juanita was speaking.

"Do you think of her often?" "Well..."Steve hesitated.

"Let go, Steve, learn to let go!"

Let go? I thought to myself. Let go!! Are you kidding me? Not on your life, Juanita. Steve will NOT let go. I will not let him. Love is forever – beyond the world of betrayal and heartbreak, beyond the pale of time and place, beyond the realm of life and death – I was together with Steve in life – and here I am together with him in death too.

Nemesis

Silence. A deep, deep, death-like silence. What did I expect? It was the middle of the night, but I couldn't rest. I had to warn Rosalyn – her life was in grave danger. I made my way along the stony path, through the rusty gate, and onto the highway. At this time of the night, there was very little traffic, so I was able to reach Rosalyn's apartment easily.

She was fast asleep. Her lashes dark on her still wet cheeks. The twin bed in the room – my bed – lay empty. She was wearing the beautiful locket our mother had given us on our sixteenth birthday. Only now, it seemed a lifetime ago.

As identical twins, we had been inseparable from the beginning. And when our wealthy Mom had remarried, we had sought refuge in each other.

Some years later, Mom died after a brief illness, and Rosalyn won a scholarship to a prestigious college. I was left alone with our stepfather.

I thought he loved us as his own children, but I was terribly wrong, as I learned to my cost.

I wrote a letter to Rosalyn about how I suspected our stepfather of all the freak accidents that kept happening to me and kept it safely in my locket.

I stood looking down at her, wordlessly.

My yearning to reach her was so intense that she woke up. Under her pillow lay my locket. As she tearfully clasped it, the latch opened. Out tumbled my letter. I saw her turn pale as she read it, and then I saw the resolve in her eyes. It did not take rocket science to see that our stepfather wanted us out of the way to take over Mom's property.

She called up her detective friend and spoke briefly. She hurriedly dressed in my favourite white dress and made her way to our stepfather's house.

She knocked repeatedly.

"Who is there in the middle of the night?"

When he opened the door, his eyes almost jumped out of their sockets.

"Marilyn! "

"Yes, Marilyn!" she said.

"No!" His voice was slurred.

He had been drinking as usual.

"How can that be?" he said drunkenly. "When I, myself mixed the overdose of sleeping pills in your milkshake!"

"Payback time!" Rosalyn whispered softly.

"I killed you once, I can kill you again!"

As he lunged at her, the lights came on. Detective Denvers with his team came out of hiding.

"Thanks for the confession, Mr. Murderer."

As he handcuffed our stepfather, Detective Denvers pulled a handkerchief from his pocket and gave it to Rosalyn, whose eyes were streaming with tears.

I could have sworn, she could see me. I saw her lips form the words, "Thank you!" I could see her smile through her tears.

As l made my way back to my own apartment - my grave - it was almost morning.

Mission accomplished, I could finally rest in peace.

The Graveyard Shift

It was already dusk when Thelma entered the building. As usual, she headed for the top floor. Only one elevator was working – the others were out of order but that did not bother her.

She had to be there from dusk to dawn – in fact, as soon as the sun set to the time it rose again – what her colleagues had called, the Graveyard Shift. Only now, it seemed a lifetime ago.

The fact that the building was falling to pieces, was largely abandoned and in line for demolition to make way for a swanky new mall and residential complexes, didn't upset her in the least either; nor did the fact that she was the only one on her floor. She knew a lot of people would be spooked by this, but it didn't bother her. As usual, she stood by the massive French window and let the cold air sweep over her. She was reminded of the words, 'where the wind's like a whetted knife'- it certainly was for it seemed to go right through her.

As usual her thoughts went to Malcolm: their whirlwind romance, their engagement, her giving him the Power of Attorney over her vast estate, Malcolm pleading with her to keep their engagement a secret just a while longer. Her twin, Wilma, had been abroad and had missed all the excitement. All she had told her was, "Wilma, I have some wonderful news to share!"

She smiled as she thought about their uncommon names – her parents had thought they were expecting twin boys and had named them – Thomas and William in advance. When the girls had been born, the obvious choice was Thelma and Wilma!

Then Malcolm had brought her here, to this very floor.

"Once this building is demolished and the mall and residential complex comes up, our penthouse is going to be right here," he had said.

He had helped an ecstatic Thelma onto the ledge.

"Be careful," he had said, "The safety wire netting is gone, only the railing remains. Here, hold my hand. See this will be the view from our bedroom window."

As she happily climbed up, the wind hit her. Malcolm held her protectively. She happily leaned against him.

"Time to say goodbye!" he had said suddenly as he pushed her over the ledge. Her scream was carried away by the wind.

Her death was written off as suicide. Malcolm's name never even came up.

An inconsolable Wilma had been comforted by who else but Malcolm. Malcolm - suave, handsome, irresistible - the only son of their father's business partner. She had no idea that Thelma had even been acquainted with Malcolm. The pattern of the whirlwind romance and action replay began. He had swept Wilma off her feet, too.

Thelma knew a leopard can never change its spots. He would be here soon with Wilma.

Then she heard the elevator creak to a halt. She heard voices. Sure enough, it was Malcolm with Wilma.

"Once this building is demolished and the mall and residential complex comes up," he was saying, "Our penthouse is going to be right here."

He climbed up onto the ledge, and as he turned to help Wilma up on the ledge, he gasped. He thought he saw a shimmering outline of Thelma.

"Oh my God! Thelma! How can that be? When I, myself..." he stopped, but the damage was done. Wilma looked up. Thelma was certain Wilma could see her. Before Malcolm could recover, Wilma's shock turned to grim resolve. She pushed hard.

"Goodbye, Malcolm – from Thelma and me! "

Taken completely by surprise, Malcolm lost his balance. The wind carried away his scream as he hurtled down to his death.

Wilma looked in Thelma's direction. Thelma was certain she could see her.

"I love you, Thelma. You've saved my life."

As she turned to go, tears streaming down her cheeks, Thelma followed her.

She no longer needed to come here. Her duty was over – she could now go from the Graveyard Shift to the graveyard, where she belonged.

Finally, at peace.

The Recruit

"This is the second time that you have been sent to the Correction Facility," the instructor's voice was cold. "Why is it so difficult for you to learn the basics?"

Of course, l had no answer. None of the students did. I stole a glance at Veronica. She was looking down, her gaze fixed on the ground below her feet. She and l were the only 'repeaters'.

The instructor handed out the time-table. "Classes begin at dusk," he said. "Theory and Practical."

He gave me a withering glance.

"And don't be late! Oh, excuse me! You are already late!" He laughed uproariously at his own joke.

Nobody said anything. We were used to his PJs. Morosely, Veronica and l wandered to my apartment. The fact that it was at the very edge of the facility and that the boundary wall was broken didn't help. A huge vacant ground lay adjoining the road that ran alongside the boundary wall. This area had been taken over by the rowdy boys of the area. They played all kinds of games, and the only thing common in all their games was the screaming and shouting. Sometimes, they jumped over the wall and continued their games in our facility. With no one to stop them, they had a field day. I could hardly hear myself think!

Veronica gazed at me, despondently. "What are we going to do, Steve?"

All of seventeen, about my age, she always deferred to me. She always sought my opinion and advice on everything. Both of us had moved in recently. I had moved in three months before her and we were still getting used to the place.

Mr. Phillips glided up to us. He was one of the oldest residents. "Fifty years!" he used to say proudly. He lived in one of the biggest plots in the middle of the facility.

"Now, don't worry," he said kindly. "You'll soon get used to your new status and duties."

"I'm not able to concentrate", said Veronica tearfully. "I miss my family."

"Well, they do come and see you, don't they? And look at the beautiful flowers they bring."

It was okay for Mr. Phillips to speak. Most of his relatives were here anyway.

He glided away.

I turned to Veronica. Together, we went through the Instructions for Beginners.

1. Remember who you are – new status.
2. Remember your duty - show them who the boss is.
3. They should actually fear coming to the facility.
4. Begin with once a week success and move to once a day success.
5. VERY IMPORTANT: Stop feeling sorry for yourself or for anyone else.

It's pretty simple to read but awfully difficult to carry out.

At dusk, we all assembled in the tiny garden in front of Mr. Phillips apartment.

The instructor, Mr. Gustavus Gordon (everyone called him Ghastly Gordon) began. "Good evening, everyone. Or should l say EVERYBODY- if you excuse the pun!"

Again, he laughed uproariously. Everyone joined in. Everyone, except Veronica and me.

"Remember your status."

Predictably, he turned to me. "Tell the others how you came to live here. No dramatics, please."

"Well, l was riding my bike, and l was singing along with the music in my earphones…" I began.

"I thought l said no dramatics."

"Okay. So here l was speeding along when a truck hit me from the back and flung me on the road."

"You weren't wearing a helmet, were you?" asked Billy, who had joined us last week.

"How could l wear headphones AND a helmet?" I wryly commented.

Everyone laughed.

"As l was saying, I was flung violently on the road. There was a searing pain, a blinding flash of light, and then nothing."

I explained how the police, the ambulance, the medics, had done a fine job; how my family, especially my mom, had wept hysterically. Finally, l was 'laid to rest' in the vacant plot at the edge of the facility near the boundary wall.

All the new residents explained how they had come to live here. No one used the word 'interred' – too high brow; or 'buried'- too pedestrian. We preferred 'came to live here.' It wasn't grammatically correct as none of us were alive, but it was a laudable euphemism.

Ghastly Gordon had taken it upon himself to teach us how to scare people – some of us, especially Victoria, and l were reluctant learners. Now we were being instructed yet again.

Mona Darling was the guest of honour and was being facilitated as she had scared a middle-aged woman witless. One moment, the woman had been taking a shortcut through our facility (we never referred to it as our cemetery – too depressing), humming to herself and the next moment she was shrieking 'like an express train going through a tunnel' – Mona's words, not mine.

Mona Darling was explaining her feat…"so when l smiled, she smiled back. Then l began to disappear a little at a time – first my hands and feet, then most of my body, then a part of my face, until only my smile was left…"

The crowd went ballistic – they laughed and cheered and clapped.

"But that was Wilma of the Whatever You Want Store," I said. "She always used to give us peppermint and chewing gum."

"You again!" said Ghastly Gordon angrily. "You have to stop feeling sorry for people."

I shrank into the corner of a white apartment (actually a grave – we called all the graves, apartments), too mortified to face anyone. Ghastly Gordon went on and on. My mind began to wander. I hardly paid attention to what he was saying.

Then, another Star Performer began to speak. It was David Doornail (as in dead as a door nail!)

"Last night," he said, "When the crusty old curmudgeon, Col. Fanthome was passing by…" and he went on and on.

There were two other speakers. After every speaker, Ghastly Gordon looked pointedly at me. Then he began speaking again. He emphasized stealth, secrecy, and the element of surprise.

"They must not suspect a thing. They must be lulled into a false sense of security."

The same old rhetoric.

"Practical 1 today," he finally concluded with a ghoulish smirk.

My assignment was to scare the first person who walked on the road that ran along the boundary wall after sunset. I lay in wait, tense as usual. I sat on the broken wall, balancing myself like a cat. Then I heard whistling. It was Rowdy Ralston, the football player and the campus bully. I gave a growl. Only it came out as a squeal. Without looking up, he flung a stone in my direction. "Bloody cat! I hate cats!" he said and resumed whistling as he continued walking.

My score: 00/100.

***

The next evening, I lay in wait again. Around 7.00 p.m., I heard footsteps. It was Gladys – the dimpled five-year-old and her mom. The moppet used to rush to me whenever she saw me, shrieking with delight, her golden curls awry. "Steve! Steve!" and lift her arms to be picked up.

Now, how could l scare them?

My score: 00/100.

***

Day 3: I sat there morosely. Clearly, I was not cut out to be a ghost. I had received a real yelling.

"Who do you think you are? Casper, the Friendly Ghost?"

He had yelled at Veronica, too. "Who do you think you are? Wendy, the Good Little Witch?"

So why do l have to scare people? Why can't l live a laid-back life (if you excuse the pun)? I thought to myself. Of course, there were benefits. If l cleared Level 1, I would get to leave the boundary of the facility up to a five kilometre radius. Level 2 meant a ten kilometre radius and Level 3 (it was the top grade - like Black Belt) would mean l could go anywhere l liked.

Just then, l heard a conversation - voices l recognized. Who should be coming down the road but Rowdy Ralston with Monika on his arm. Monika! I had always wanted to date Monika. She was not only a cheerleader but also the undisputed queen of our campus. Of course, she had preferred Ralston to me. He was in the football team, had a faster, sleeker motorcycle – a Harley Davidson, no less, and more importantly, his dad was stinking rich. I heard her dulcet tone and Ralston's responses. I could imagine her fluttering her eyelashes, and l could imagine too his self-satisfied look, like a cat that had gotten all the cream.

Suddenly, I was filled with rage – unlike anything I had known before. It was like a fire raging inside me, burning me up – only there was nothing to burn. Why was life so unfair? I gave a howl of rage and frustration. To my utter astonishment, they stopped dead in their tracks.

"D...Did you hear that?" Monika asked fearfully.

Both looked up. They saw a cloudy representation of a human form – me!

"Oh my God!" This was Ralston. Not so cocky any longer. Then they were running helter-skelter! Absolutely terrified! By the time I recovered, they had disappeared. One of Monika's heels lay abandoned on the road! Then it struck me - I had actually scared someone!! But this truly sank in when Ghastly Gordon and the others clapped and cheered. Good Heavens! I had an audience! I didn't know what to say – but I needn't have worried. I didn't have to say anything. Ghastly Gordon and the others couldn't stop congratulating me. I cleared Level 1 with flying colours!

***

Guess who the Guest of Honour is tomorrow? That's right, it's me! While I prepare my speech for tomorrow, my mind goes into overdrive planning my extra classes for Veronica and my POA (Plan Of

Action) for clearing Level 2.

EVERYTHING ELSE

The Homecoming

Had it really only been fifty minutes since she got here? It felt so much longer. She glanced up at the wall clock again. Had it stopped? She would have gladly come at dawn – in any case, she had been unable to sleep a wink - but for security reasons - she would not have been allowed to enter. She was unable to stand in one place. She began pacing restlessly up and down the crowded platform. She felt about as calm as a cat on a hot tin roof. She did not even attempt to make a conversation with the other people there, although everyone was chatting animatedly.

The whole place was decorated – it wore a festive look. Spic and span, the floor shone like glass. Welcome banners and garlands of flowers had transformed the place. Young girls, barely out of their teens – probably sweethearts and young wives; stood with older people – probably brothers, sisters, fathers, mothers like herself. Even young children with their teddies clutched to them – jostled for space. There were tall military men resplendent in their starched uniforms, the Guard of Honour, the Welcoming Committee, and even a band. The whole place looked like an army cantonment.

After all, they were welcoming the war heroes home! The Military Police tried to manage the crowd, but it was an uphill task. Excitement, anticipation, and joy filled the air; it was palpable. She herself was on pins and needles.

She had not seen Jeremy for over a year. In fact, from the time he had left to fight a 'righteous war'. So tall, so handsome in his splendid new uniform – how proud she was of him! He was the one bright spot in her otherwise dull, uneventful life.

The desire for fame and respect had been like a drug in her bloodstream – destroying every rational thought. A single mother with no great qualifications or job, her neighbours thought her about as relevant as a fur coat in the Sahara Desert. It was through her son that her obsession for fame could be realized. She would be treated with respect and admiration. When he had enlisted, she had seen the change in the neighbours' attitude. The craving for respect and fame permeated every facet of her being, spreading like a deadly poison in her veins...

Her son, always caring, protective, and loving, had worried about leaving her alone. She had hugged him - as usual, dwarfed by his size.

"Now, Jem, don't you worry about anything," she had said. "I'll look after Rover and take him for walks.

I'll take care of myself. I'll take care of the house. You just follow orders and bring home a lot of medals." She had a new display shelf made right on the mantelpiece of the living room - just perfect for his medals. She pictured him putting them on display (she was not tall enough to reach that high) and the resulting euphoria was once again like a drug - wonderful, uplifting, heady. She pictured the faces of the neighbours – especially the much decorated and much respected Colonel Cruthers and that feeling beat any drug in existence.

Jem had written every week. How she had bragged to the neighbours! Suddenly, they had started listening to her. They had actually begun giving her the attention and respect she craved. What would happen when Jeremy would be a decorated officer with his name in the papers? What would happen when they saw Jem, tall and handsome beside her, standing and smiling with his medals? She shivered with anticipation. She was already on a 'high'.

Suddenly the letters had stopped coming. Without him or his letters, her life was about as exciting as a pandemic lock down. Silence for six months. Must be some emergency, or maybe one emergency after another, she had consoled herself. After all, he was on the war front. Who could tell what the brave young men were facing? That's what she also said to the solicitous inquires of the neighbours.

Then came the telegram from the Army Headquarters – her son would be on this train bringing the war heroes home today. She had been overwhelmed with relief and happiness. She had shown the telegram to all her neighbours and slept with it under her pillow – getting up many times in the night to read and re-read it.

Since then, she had been in a fever of anticipation – unable to eat or sleep. Maria, her best friend, had wanted to come to the railway station with her. She had known Jem since he was a toddler – but she had not wanted to share the return of her hero. She had even bought herself a new dress. Maria had said, "Wow! You look terrific! Smart enough to be a war hero's mom!"

Of course, she couldn't have brought Rover – dogs were not allowed. She knew the neighbours were busy arranging a grand welcome party. The entire building was being decorated. After all it was a matter of pride for the whole community – a war hero from their own neighbourhood! Even that snooty Norma, who had usually looked through her, behaved as if they had been childhood friends.

Finally, she heard the whistle - the crowd cheered, the band began playing. Then suddenly, everything exploded in a kaleidoscope of sound, colour, and chaos! The train, festooned with garlands, had arrived!

What a tremendous homecoming – shouts of delight, laughter, tears, hugs, kisses...

She desperately looked around for Jem. He would surely be among the tallest. She ran her eyes over the rapidly thinning crowd. Everyone was in a hurry to get home with their hero. Where was Jem? She longed to hear his booming voice, longed to see her tall, handsome son, longed to be enveloped in his bear hug...

Now, only some young men on crutches and wheelchairs were left. Their loved ones, with the Military Police in attendance, were helping them as they slowly and carefully traversed the rapidly emptying platform. Her handsome Jem would have towered over the crowd. Had Jem not boarded this train? She wondered whom to ask. Should she ask the officers on the Welcoming Committee, the ones with the lists? Or the officers at the counter, 'May l help you?' Or the Military Police? She was in a quandary. She still clutched the telegram like a talisman in her hand. She wished she had brought Maria with her. She was turning away in disappointment, her eyes clouding when someone touched her arm. She turned. It was a man in a wheelchair – half his face was swathed in bandages, his legs covered with a blanket.

A hoarse, rasping voice, a voice she did not recognize - said, "It's me, Mom. I brought home the medals."

Making a Difference

Do you ever get the feeling that you are starting on the wrong foot and that you are a centipede? Well, that's the feeling l got when l entered my Chief's office that day. I was six months into the Metropolitan Police Force, and the Chief still regarded me as a sixth finger on one of his immaculately manicured hands. I had topped my class at the Police Academy, had several medals for martial arts, sports, and even boxing, but all that seemed quite irrelevant as far as the Chief was concerned.

"You are here to chase, catch, and arrest criminals – not mollycoddle them! Haven't l told you that more times than the hair on your shaggy head?" were his favourite lines to me

The other three who had joined with me were doing remarkably well. Every other day, there was a violent arrest, and the law breaker was brought in bruised, bloody, and broken. The Chief loved this.

"Well done!" he would say. "We have to cleanse society of this vermin."

He would always have a word of praise for the police officer making the arrest, looking pointedly at me. If looks could kill, l would have died many times over.

"This is a society on the boil - ready to spill over into violence. We need to prevent that. We need to be feared," he always cautioned us.

How could l tell him, l was fighting fate and my own DNA – my father had been a belligerent, violent man, always beating up Mom, my kid brother and me on the slightest reason or no reason at all. We had some peace when she divorced him and vowed to keep us away from his violent influence.

"My sons will not grow up to be even a bit like him!" she swore, and under her gentle upbringing, we had grown up into fine young men. I had joined the police force, and my kid brother was in medical school.

"But surely we can be friendly with the people?" l had asked once asked my Chief.

"Yeah! As friendly as cats are with mice! "

He had laughed uproariously.

That morning, l was particularly nervous. The day before, I had caught a kid peddling drugs. I had not arrested him but had handed him over to his school counsellor. She had been truly grateful.

"Dalton has never stepped out of line before – he has always got straight A's. It's just that his mom's cancer has seriously disturbed him…"

"Glad to be of help, Miss."

"Melissa, please, officer. I'm glad to see that police officers have hearts, too!"

I smiled. I always believed in giving second chances.

To add to my list of growing misdemeanors, just that morning I had let off a girl who had been speeding.

"Officer, my grandma is seriously ill," she had said with tears in her eyes. How could I give her a ticket?

My Chief had a notoriously low boiling point at the best of times. That day, when I walked in feeling as calm as a cat on a hot tin roof, he looked like a volcano about to erupt. He turned to me.

"Okay, Boy Scout, go and make arrests. Do you think you are here to win a Mr. Congeniality contest? Well, let me tell you, you are not! You are here to locate, engage, and destroy all criminals. Remember, fear is the key."

I knew better than to say that I wanted to make a difference, I wanted to separate the first-time offenders from the hardened criminals. I knew he wouldn't listen – he always treated me the way Cinderella's stepmother must have treated her. No wonder I could never jump into the fray but always remained hovering on the fringe. Don't get me wrong. I loved my job, but l wanted to avoid unnecessary violence.

Feeling like an extra in a multi – starrer movie, l slunk out unobtrusively. I looked back on my performance so far. Was l really making a difference? Okay, so I was winning hearts – but were criminals really scared of me? I had no answer.

I decided to go check on Dalton – actually, l wanted to see Melissa again. She seemed kind and gentle - the qualities that always attracted me; the qualities I had always admired, the qualities that reminded me of Mom.

When l got to the school, I felt instinctively that something was very wrong. There was no one at the entrance, no one at the reception. The glass panelled cubicle was empty. The classrooms were empty too. Where was everyone? Then l heard a whimpering. I tiptoed to the stage entrance of the hall that served as an auditorium. A function had obviously been in progress. But what was this? From the half open door, l could see the teachers and students standing shell-shocked while a gunman stood on the stage, holding Melissa by the neck. "One move and she gets shot!" he intoned. He had a gun, just inches from her beautiful, terrified face.

Then something strange happened – the hall, the students, the teachers, even Melissa disappeared. All l could see was the gunman. With an ear–shattering yell, the kind l had heard on TV, l kicked the door fully open and flung myself on the gunman. The expression on his face was ludicrous. The gun flew out of his hand and two well- aimed kicks had him on the floor. To say he was shocked out of his wits would be an understatement. I took out my so far unused handcuffs and handcuffed his limp, unresisting hands behind his back. As he lay prone at my feet too frightened to even move, the world gradually swam into focus. The click of the handcuffs seemed to have broken a spell. Melissa rushed forward and clung to my one free arm. The principal recovered enough to say, "Wow! Kindergarten Cop! That was amazing! Well done!"

And the hall erupted into frenzied cheering. The students and teachers could not stop clapping.

Finally, I was making a difference!

B4U

As soon as Harriet entered the building, she headed to the seventh floor. The rickety elevator opened into a garishly lit, carpeted lobby. The entire floor was taken up by B4U - the happening place with four Bs - Bar , Barbecue, Billiards, and Bingo (a euphemism for all card games, mainly gambling). She adjusted her low cut shimmering satin gown and headed straight for the bar. Bill, the bartender, gave his usual cheery greeting. Even though it was just a few minutes past 8.00 p.m., the place, as usual, was already full of smoke, chatter, and bonhomie. This was the saving grace of the seedy building reputed to be owned by 'The Mob'. Situated in a once upmarket area, its street now boasted of boarded-up establishments, seedy joints, unkempt driveways, and broken pavements. The rest of the floors were taken up by offices of down-at-heel lawyers; offices of wheeler-dealers offering everything from model assignments, television and film roles to plush jobs; some guest houses, massage parlours and two- roomed apartments. There was also a gym on the ground floor.

Harriet helped out at the bar from 8.00 p.m. to 12.30 a.m., the busiest time. It allowed Bill to take a much needed break and gave the regulars some eye candy and someone to talk to. Only three months into the job, Harriet was already very popular. Her genius for mixing drinks was rivalled only by her talent for providing a sympathetic ear. She always remained friendly but always strictly and tantalizingly out of reach. The two bouncers who remained just out of sight kept a strict vigilant watch on her.

The four piece band usually played on weekends. So, there was relative peace. As she took her normal lime and soda, Billy marvelled once again at how a teetotaler like her could mix such an amazing concoction of drinks. She sat on her usual stool and waved at the regulars whose eyes lit up on seeing her.

"This place could get addictive," said Harriet. "I never knew it could grow on me. When l took up this job to earn extra money for my college fees, l was really hesitant."

"Anyone would think you've been doing this all your life," said Bill admiringly. "And the icing on the cake is that you are a quick learner, H. I'm sure glad you are here. You know many people wonder what a lovely young girl like you is doing in an unlovely place like this."

Harriet ran her eyes over the fast filling place.

"No, not unlovely, just different, B."

Bill laughed. They had taken to calling each other 'H' and 'B'. Around middle age, Bill always looked out for her.

"Look, Mo has turned up again! I think he's smitten by you!"

Mo the Mower (always known to mow down his victims) was the Mob's hit man. Rarely seen in public, he was wanted by the police in half a dozen states. No one could or would positively identify him. Here he was safe - after all the seventh floor was his own haven of refuge.

Harriet turned to look. Mo was indeed staring fixedly in her direction.

"I think after you fixed his arm and gave him the soothing concoction, he fell under your spell."

Harriet smiled. "Anyone would have helped a hurt and bleeding person."

"Only this hurt and bleeding person had a deep knife wound. He had just knifed a police informer and flung him from that corner window just before you came in that day."

"Don't believe everything you hear," said Harriet.

Bill laughed. "It's your cool, non- judgmental attitude that really won him over."

Harriet smiled.

"I say," said Bill. "Look at those two morose looking gentlemen in the far corner. If they aren't enjoying themselves, why are they here?"

Harriet looked. The two gentlemen looked really unhappy, sitting listlessly and nursing their drinks.

Harriet laughed. "Well, it takes all kinds."

"That's another thing I like about you, you are always so cool and matter of fact."

Mo nudged up to the bar. Without a word, Harriet mixed him his favourite Bloody Mary. As she handed it to him, she gave him two yellow paper napkins.

"To help you keep your hands dry," she smiled.

As Mo went back to his corner, Harriet sat down suddenly, holding her head.

"B, can I take this evening off? I am not feeling too well. Besides, today is the last date to submit my assignment."

Harriet rarely asked for leave.

"By all means, H, go right ahead. I'll manage."

As Harriet walked out, she saw the two gentlemen in the far corner get to their feet. She headed for the ground floor and took a cab home.

The papers next day were full of the dramatic seventh floor arrest of Mo the Mower, the Mob's hit man.

She turned to her phone. It was full of congratulatory messages - her boss - the Police Chief, the 'two morose gentlemen', Dan and Jack of the Crime Branch, and almost all her colleagues in the department. They especially commended her for the yellow napkins as a means of identification.

Ah well, thought Harriet, as she picked a scarlet gown for that evening, being an undercover agent wasn't all that bad.

The Heart of the Matter

Prologue : Circa 2020-21

I sat on the bench at the deserted waterfront. The inside of my collar was wet, and beads of perspiration stood out on my forehead. I was immune to the cool breeze from the river.

Every few minutes, as of their own accord, my eyes darted furtively around me. So far, no one. The riverfront remained deserted. I gazed unseeingly at the river.

Then suddenly, as if out of nowhere, four men materialized. They were all about the same age - late twenties or thereabouts. They were tall, lanky, rather pale; wearing identical white button-down shirts, tight–fitting black suits, and black ties.

"Victor?" asked one.

I nodded, too overwhelmed to speak.

"Godfrey."

"Gordon."

"Gustavus."

"Gore."

Were they kidding me? Wasn't this the name of a boy in a poem by WB Rands? The boy who wouldn't shut the door? I remember learning it in school. Was it a veiled warning - for the boy in the poem was nearly dispatched to Singapore. Or was it their ham-handed attempt at humour? Who could tell? Needless to say, l had never felt less like smiling, let alone laughing.

They didn't attempt to shake hands but gazed at me, unblinking with their identical expressionless black eyes.

"How do you want it?" one of them finally said.

"How do I want what?" I croaked.

"The money, of course."

"Do you have an account? "

"An offshore one? "

They seemed to be speaking in tandem.

"No, no. Of course not."

I didn't say that my only onshore account was badly over drawn. The manager had already given 'friendly advice', and l was also defaulting on my mortgage payments.

They exchanged glances.

"The account will be opened."

"The money transferred."

"Keep your end of the bargain."

"You are under surveillance now."

Again, in tandem. Another attempt at humour. In normal circumstances, l would have found this hugely funny - but the circumstances were anything but normal.

Too tense to speak, I merely nodded. My hand shook as l tried to light a cigarette. One of them gave me a withering glance and lit it for me. Then, as suddenly as they had come, they were gone!

Had I imagined it all? The river mirrored the myriad lights as the sky turned purple. Stars began to twinkle in the velvet black. But l was blind to the beauty. The cold night air soothed me. My breathing returned to normal. I flung away my un-smoked cigarette. I swallowed. My mouth seemed full of ashes. My legs were still unsteady as I got to my feet.

A momentous decision had been made.

The Present:

I clutched the keys of the latest model of the sports car. My son would be delighted. It's true I was seeing little of him these days, but then again, l was seeing little of my entire family. It had not always been like this. We had been very close - Victoria, my high-school sweetheart, and I had been happily married for eighteen years. My son Vincent was a good child - always getting good grades and a good sports person.

This new phase had started some time ago. I don't recall the exact date, but I clearly remember the Christmas party at my flat. The living room was full of laughter and excitement - my family and friends celebrating Christmas. Of course, Freddy was there. Everyone called him Freddy-the-Fixer. He was good looking in a rather slick way. Divorced, with a steady stream of girlfriends, he drove a Lamborghini and lived in a penthouse. He was nothing like my other friends. Victoria didn't like him one bit. I had met him at the Port where I work. I sign the permits that let the cargo of ships into the country. A responsible job - a job I was committed to.

"How long do you intend living in that hovel you call a home?" he asked as we enjoyed a quiet smoke after the party. "I thought you wanted to put Vincent through college."

Before l could react, he spelled out the deal. All l had to do was to ensure the consignment marked 'Valentine's Day,' was not checked thoroughly at the dock. There were baubles, knick- knacks, bracelets with tiny dangling pink hearts, the sort of things kids love. The kind of money l would make left me dumbstruck. So why was the money being paid out? This was nothing but a crude bribe. Well, the tiny pink hearts contained banned drugs. Drugs, that would spell disaster for the youth. They were instantly habit–forming with terrible results.

I was no match for the smooth-talking Freddie-the-Fixer. Besides, he played on my emotional side and lurking ambition to get rich. Needless to say, l was an easy prey.

The first consignment I signed, my hand trembled.

What the heck, I told myself, it's the way of the world.

We moved into our new penthouse soon after. I stopped meeting my extended family and old friends. They never said a word, but I was unable to face them or even attempt to answer the questions in their eyes.

Victoria and I no longer had long chats about everyone and everything. It was weeks ago that I had held her close. She now had that permanent look of bewilderment on her face. She looked completely lost. I knew she would soon ask me how we had got so rich in such a short time. I was putting off that moment as long as l could. However, Vincent took to our new lifestyle like a fish to water. He loved our new penthouse, our new Audi, the branded clothes, the fancy places he could take his friends with the generous allowance I gave him.

The sports car was his birthday present. He had no idea what l had gotten for him. I was planning a big bash for his birthday. I reached our apartment building and gave my keys to the attendant. He would park the car. I was too excited and in too much of a hurry. I wanted to see the expression on my son's face -

unbelieving, awed, delighted – the way he had reacted when I had bought him his new bicycle.

I went up to our penthouse wondering why the elevator was not moving fast enough. I kept looking at the floors as we rose higher and higher. I glared at people getting on and off at various floors. I rushed out the moment the door opened.

I have my own key but I love knocking so that Vic can open the door with her sweet smile. I raised my hand to knock, but what was this? The door was ajar!

"Vic!" l shouted. "Vinny! Where are you? "

There was no answer. The master bedroom was empty.

I went up to Vincent's room.

"Guess what l got for you…" I began but stopped mid-sentence. That door was ajar too. Lying on the carpet was my wife, and comatose on the bed, my son. In his half open hand, I could just glimpse a bracelet - a bracelet with a tiny pink heart…

An Idea Whose Time Has Come

Helen was on tenterhooks as she headed to her office that day. This entire floor housed the offices and workstations of FM Radio- an immensely popular radio station.

The building itself was a landmark. Set in huge grounds, there was a lot of greenery. The entire ground floor was taken up by 'Second Innings' – a swanky old age home. The huge reception area had dozens of receptionists behind gleaming glass partitions, a dozen inquiry counters with the inevitable, 'May I Help You?' and a dozen more special counters.

The floor housed one roomed and two roomed self-contained apartments with every amenity imaginable, three dining areas, and two recreation areas.

The first floor housed the gym, the spa, the library, and the reading rooms.

The third and fourth housed 'Health City' a fully equipped state of the art twenty-bedded hospital, operating rooms, doctors' chambers with every modern amenity.

The fifth had call centres and the sixth corporate offices.

Helen felt her floor was the busiest. She greeted her boss Clarence 'Cherry' Chambers and headed to her cubicle that she shared with her friend, Sally. They hosted 'Yesterday, Today and Tomorrow,' an immensely popular programme that played songs of yesteryear, the latest popular numbers and the songs of up and coming struggling artistes. Sally, individually handled 'Sally's Solutions' that dealt with everything from finding a flat, a flat mate, a holiday destination, the best place to dine and even scholarships - you name it and Sally had a solution.

Helen herself handled 'Heart to Heart with Helen' – where she gave a sympathetic ear and played Agony Aunt.

Helen headed to the conference room on the same floor. Yes, everything was ready for the weekend ANCHORS (an acronym for Anchors - reps from the seventh floor, Newbies - the reps from the gym on the first floor and call centres on the fifth floors, Corporate reps from the sixth floor, the Hospital reps from the third floor, the Oppenheimers, the representatives from the fourth floor, the Regals - the reps from the professors from the second floor and the owners, and the Senior Citizens - reps from the ground floor).

This was a part of their much-appreciated KYN – Know Your Neighbour Campaign. And it worked like a charm.

"After all, we are all one big family," Walter Hauffmann, the senior partner and a retired bureaucrat, would often say. A view shared by almost all the bureaucrats, doctors, and lawyers. Many of them lived in 'Second Innings' but were extremely active and voluble. Cherry, her boss, was also a retired bureaucrat committed to broad casting. There was a fair representation of almost all professions and callings.

Ever since the new Peoples Popular Party had been elected, they had witnessed a slow and systematic stifling of democracy. The first to succumb, surprisingly, was the media. From being a Watchdog of Democracy it had been reduced to the Lapdog of the Ruling Party. Day in and day out, the News Channels belted out propaganda.

Soon, any kind of criticism of the government was termed anti-national, and the bewildered dissenter was locked up on charges of sedition. Even party workers who did not toe the line were given the third degree. A growing group of concerned citizens had decided to do something about it. And that is what they were doing. Drawn from all twenty-six districts, there were people from all walks of life. Their aim was only to ensure a decimating defeat to the present government in the next elections and to restore democracy to their beleaguered land. The whole operation was modelled on the French Resistance - but with one crucial difference. Unlike the French Resistance, it was not underground. It was very much in your face. Right under the nose of the authorities, this bustling, busy building was a power-keg of resistance, destined to release their beloved country from the stranglehold of the present dispensation and relegate to oblivion the enemies of democracy. They wanted to bring back their vibrant democracy.

With the next elections perilously close, every meeting was an important link in the series. So far, so good. With a partisan police force and government employees who were nothing more than HMV – His Master's Voice – of course the voice of the Supreme Commander – the Supremo who had risen from humble beginnings to dominate over all; they had to exercise the utmost caution.

Today's meeting was greatly anticipated. At precisely 10.00, the participants filed in, smiling, friendly, optimistic. Reps from all twenty-six districts were there. The Automatic Voting Machines were supposed to have been tampered with - no matter which button the voter pressed, the machine recorded a vote for the ruling party. The reps had to report on the success of restoring the machines to their original un-tampered version. How they managed it was left to their ingenuity.

Finally, Walter and Cherry, the two chairpersons, called the meeting to order. The representatives of all twenty-six districts were seated in alphabetical order – from Alpha to Zeus.

The proceedings were begun by Walter who began with the usual opening- the password first (not all the people who worked here were members of the Resistance) – 'I am an idea whose time has come.'

Maurice from Alpha District began, "It was a microchip inserted in the AVMs that caused all the problems."

He explained how he and his team had been able to remove these microchips and restore the AVMs to their original system.

As the others took turns to talk about inserted wires, changes in default settings, cutting of the connection between the buttons, and the outcome, Helen's mind began to wander. She thought of how her father, a renowned poet and Professor of History, had been arrested on charges of being an anti–national for an innocuous post on history. Sally's brother, of the Editor's Guild, had been detained for protesting against the illegal detention of one of their members. No one knew their whereabouts.

Helen finally came back to the present when Zeke from Zeus District was making his concluding remarks.

"So that takes care of all the AVMs. Let the election come - the ruling party will know to their cost what the people really want! They will be wiped out!"

Thunderous applause greeted this statement.

Walter finally took the microphone and after the usual appreciative comments said, "They tried to bury us but they did not know that we are seeds and soon this beautiful land made arid by them will be lush green again! Democracy and human rights will reign supreme once more!"

Just then, the door opened. Everyone looked up – who would dare enter this closed door meeting? It was the Police Chief - Franklin!

Walter recovered first.

"Welcome, Chief Franklin!" he said as if the chief attending their meetings was an everyday occurrence.

"We were just discussing the progress of our sister concern – Body and Soul - the committees in each district to promote theatre, public speaking, visits to libraries and art galleries – to bring all citizens into the mainstream and provide hands-on aid to the deserving."

This, of course, was the brilliant front of the Resistance.

The Chief took the chair Helen offered, looked around, and taking the microphone from Walter said clearly and distinctly, "Not everyone in authority is a lap dog. I am an idea whose time has come."

Finally Justice

Today is the day of the landmark judgment – State vs. Senator Anthony Felton. I have to give the verdict. We all know what it is going to be - not guilty. If the lawyers get a celebrity accused to my court, the verdict is pre-determined. Money changes hands - not in the crude form of briefcases stuffed with filthy lucre, but a discreet transfer of funds to my offshore account.

It was not always like this. Fresh out of law school, among the top five, with dreams and ideals, I had truly believed I could change the world. "Injustice anywhere is a threat to justice everywhere," I had thundered in the debate that had not only won me the best speaker but also Kelly, my beautiful, sensitive batch- mate. Where had I lost my way? I can't really say. The watershed came when I let off Papa Pete, the drug smuggler against overwhelming evidence. Kelly had come to me, her eyes bright with unshed tears. "Joshua, you are not the man I married. I am leaving you."

Just like that. No melodramatic posturing, no accusations, no tears.

What's more, she left our daughter with me and walked out of our lives.

Did this affect me? More than I can say. Did it change me? No. The pittance I was making before the 'make-over' could maybe buy candy and balloons for my daughter's birthday party, not this extravagant lifestyle. I lived in a colonial style villa in the city's most exclusive neighbourhood. I drove a Lamborghini and had a beautiful yacht tucked away for parties and exclusive jaunts.

Today, I did not want to go to my court. Every time the petitioner – a young girl barely out of her teens – looked trustfully at me, I felt a pang. Was my conscience still alive? I think she was the only one who believed that Tony Felton, the rapist, would get what he deserved.

I entered the jam-packed courtroom. The buzz in the courtroom died down. Tony Felton was looking his engaging best, and the two lawyers, his lawyer and Pattie's lawyer, looked as oily and slimy as only crooked lawyers can.

The excited buzz now rose again and went up an octave higher. Pattie had entered, clad in white, her eyes downcast, her arm in a plaster cast.

As the lawyers made their concluding speeches, I glanced idly at the Statue of the blindfolded Goddess of Justice with her scales. What is she measuring? Surely not justice! And that too in my court! I felt that pang again.

The lawyers had finished.

As l cleared my throat to speak, all eyes on me, Pattie suddenly threw the plaster cast aside, whipped out a gun hidden in it, and trained it on Felton, then on both the lawyers. It was a ludicrous sight – everyone frozen into immobility. By the time they recovered, she had turned it on herself. As l cowered behind my desk, I saw inexplicably, not Pattie's face, but my daughter's... I could hear my silent scream –"Pattie! Pattie! I should be next! I am a part of this system…"

Then everything came to life! It was like watching a movie in slow motion and then in fast-forward. But as the cops swarmed the near empty courtroom, all l could see were four limp bodies, upturned chairs, an abandoned umbrella, a high heeled pump and the blood dripping everywhere - like water dripping from a rock…

Check Your Premises

All the lawns on Mentone Avenue are mowed on Wednesdays. That gave two whole days for decorations. The biggest villa, of course, belonged to Sidney Maximilian. He was celebrating his 75th birthday on Saturday.

On Saturday morning, the phone rang exactly at 8.31 a.m.

"Lt. Andrew Cartwright," l said crisply.

"Oh God! Andy! Come quickly! It's Uncle Sid!" cried Laura, her voice breaking. "Uncle Sid…"

Someone took the phone from her. It was Malcolm, Sidney Maximilian's eldest son.

"Lt Cartwright, please come at once. I think Dad's dead!"

"What!" I said. "But he was perfectly well when l saw him this morning!"

"You left around 7.30 a.m. Maria says that when she served the tea, he was perfectly well."

"I'll be right there. Don't touch anything."

I informed the homicide team and got into my cruiser with Ian MacDougal, my deputy, and raced to Sidney Maximilian's villa.

"Strange," said Ian, "He seemed fine when we saw him in the morning."

I nodded in agreement.

Malcolm met us at the door and led us to the foyer. It was crowded with his house guests.

"I hope nothing has been touched," I said.

They all shook their heads, too overwhelmed to speak. I followed Malcolm to the huge master bedroom on the ground floor. I could see preparations well underway in the massive grounds for the big bash that evening.

Sidney Maximilian lay half sitting on his bed. His teacup lay drained by the bedside table. On the window-sill sat his cat - Lady Catherine, his dog Sir Donald lay whimpering near the bed. His parrot, Madame Pollyanna, was nowhere to be seen. Then Ian shouted—Pollyanna lay still and cold between the bed and the bedside table.

"Who found Sid?" I asked.

"Norma, his nurse," said Malcolm.

I took one whiff of the teacup. "Probably poisoned."

"Oh my God!" It was Laura, "We were to celebrate his 75th birthday today."

She broke into hysterical sobs.

"Everyone had gathered here for the big bash. I saw your name on the guest list too," said Malcolm.

Everyone was looking in from the foyer, not daring to come in.

"Nothing is to be touched," I warned again. "The homicide team has been informed. They will soon be here."

I came out into the foyer.

"Please get dressed and meet me in the living room," I glanced at my watch. "In fifteen minutes. I want all the household staff here too."

Fifteen minutes later, they began filing in. Being a constant visitor, I knew most of them. Mona, his twenty-nine year old third wife, and Monica, her twin sister; Leonardo, his second wife's son; Laura, the orphaned daughter of his friend who stayed there; and Malcolm, of course.

These were the house guests. The other guests had been accommodated at the two nearby five star hotels. Thankfully, they had not been informed.

Of course, the staff, comprising Mrs. Hutchinson, the housekeeper; Norma the nurse; Gonsalves the cook; Maria the maid; were all there. Jeeves the butler was unwell and was supposed to report in the evening.

I glanced at them. "I want to speak to each one of you separately in the library."

A tsunami of protestations met my remark.

"Are you suspecting us? "

"Blood relatives?"

"Why would we want him dead?"

"I loved Sid!"

I gave them a withering glance.

"I'll be in the library. I'll call you in alphabetical order. Of course, Mona will come last of all."

Once in the library, I went over the list given to me by Malcolm.

The first to come was Gonsalves the cook. He looked shell–shocked.

I switched on my tape recorder.

"I swear I made the tea as I always do. Just the way he liked it. I also drank the remaining tea as I always do. Why would I want to kill Sir Sidney? He was so appreciative of my cooking! "

"No one is accusing you," I said placatingly. "Do you suspect anyone? "

Gonsalves, calmed, for the moment, came closer.

"It could very well be Leonardo. They never got along. They had an argument last night, too."

Next was the housekeeper, Mrs. Hutchinson. She came in, wringing her hands.

"Oh poor, Mr. Sidney," she said tearfully. "No doubt he was difficult to please, but why would anyone kill him? And his birthday too! "

"Do you suspect anyone?"

"Oh, Officer," her voice fell to a whisper. "It could be Leonardo," she came closer to my desk. "It could very well be Madame Mona. They never got along! And ever since Madame Monica has come, things have been worse – they don't even sleep in the same room anymore! We think Mr. Sidney plans to divorce her…"

Leonardo, in his mid–thirties, came in quite flustered.

"I always looked upon him as a father. Why would I want to kill him?"

"No one is accusing you, Leo," I said calmly. "Do you suspect anyone?"

He perked up at once. He clutched my arm.

"You mark my words, it's those terrible twins - Mona and Monica! Dammit! They are younger than me! And Mona is nothing but a cheap gold-digger. Besides, she hated his guts! "

Laura came in, dabbing her eyes.

"I loved Uncle Sid, "she said tearfully. "He was like a father to me. Why would I want to kill him?"

She began crying again.

"Calm down, Laura," I said. Do you suspect anyone?"

"Suspect?" A pause. "It could well be Mona. Or maybe, Leonardo…"

Malcolm was next, but before we could start, Ian informed me that the team from Police Headquarters had arrived. I told Ian to take the team to the bedroom and begin investigations while I completed my interrogation.

Malcolm, a successful investment banker, was in his forties. He looked quite distinguished. His family had not come as his wife was busy with their son's university admissions.

"I really don't know what to say," he said somberly. "He had a lot of flaws, but even after the divorce, he saw me through college."

I repeated my question, "Malcolm, do you suspect anyone?"

"Now that you ask, it is probably Mona with Monica's help, of course, or even Leonardo. Actually, Dad was going to have his new will read out. He had summoned his lawyers. Mona and Leonardo feared being left out."

Next was Maria the maid. She looked totally distraught.

"I brought the tea as usual," she said tearfully. "I swear I didn't add anything to it. Neither did Gonsalves. We shared the leftover tea in the kitchen, as usual - and we are fine…" "Do you suspect anyone?"

Maria looked up.

"It could have been Leonardo. They never got along. But most probably, it was Madame Mona. You should have seen the way they argued. Except for them, l can't think of anyone else."

Next was Monica. She breezed into the room.

"I resent this. I completely resent this! You realize you are insulting me, don't you? The Police Chief will hear of this – I am going to lodge a complaint."

"Please yourself. But as l said l am not accusing anyone – I am just making inquiries."

"I just got here a week ago. We were having a whale of a time! Why would l want to kill anyone? And Sid of all people?"

"Do you suspect anyone?"

"Well, it's not me or Mona. Why don't you ask Leonardo? And what about that goody- goody Laura?

She's there with him all the time!"

Norma, the nurse, was next. She looked completely flustered.

"I swear I had just gone to the washroom when Maria brought the tea. I was hired to look after him, not kill him!"

"Calm down," I said. "Do you suspect anyone?"

She wiped her eyes.

"It could well be Madame Mona with Monica's help..."

Now came Mona. Even at this time, she was in full makeup. She looked more like a hooker than a recently bereaved wife.

"Just because we got into arguments doesn't mean we didn't get along. We haven't been sharing our bedroom for only a week. Ever since Monica came. Poor thing is very upset. I keep her company, to cheer her up. She is going through a messy divorce. Why don't you ask Leonardo?"

We were interrupted. It was Ian.

"Can I have a word with you?"

Preliminary investigations revealed that Sid had indeed been poisoned. The medics took his body for the post-mortem and secured all the evidence - the teacup and its contents, and the parrot, Pollyanna, in separate containers. A watch had been found - wedged between the bed and the bedside table.

"That's Leonardo's watch!" shouted Mona triumphantly. "What did l tell you?"

Meanwhile, the others had come up.

"My watch!" cried Leonardo in surprise. "But where did you find it? It was lost!" There was a stunned silence.

Despite his shocked protests, Ian clapped the handcuffs on his wrists as prime suspect, on circumstantial evidence, pending further investigations, of course.

"You have the right to remain silent," he intoned. "Anything you say can be used as evidence against you."

I took my tape-recorder and took my leave as soon as our team with Leonardo had left. A lot of work had to be done. Until results of the tea sample and post-mortem results of both Sid and the parrot were in, Leonardo had to be lodged in a cell.

As l drove back, I thought to myself, how right Ayn Rand was when she famously said, 'Contradictions don't exist in nature. If you find they do, check your premises, one of them is sure to be wrong.'

Premise: In a rational world, law enforcers cannot be law breakers, let alone murderers, right? Wrong!!

First of all, who says it's a rational world?

Ever since Sid had confided that he wanted to kick out Mona and marry Laura, his fate was sealed.

Concealing my shock, I had asked, "Isn't she like your granddaughter?"

"LIKE my granddaughter but NOT ACTUALLY my granddaughter!" he had said slyly.

What about Leonardo? When his attempts to persuade Laura to become his second wife failed, he tried to molest her. That sealed his fate too!

This morning, while Sid was in the washroom, I gave Pollyanna some crackers as I usually did, but this time, I let her dip her beak into a concentrated solution of fast drying cyanide. I knew Sid always shared his tea with her. First, she dipped her beak, and then Sid took a sip.

Thus, it was only a matter of time. Dip, dip! Sip, sip! There you have the perfect murder! Besides, it was child's play to swipe Leonardo's watch on one of my numerous visits. And today, slip it between the bed and the bedside table. Clinching evidence!

As I drove back, the breeze felt cool on my fevered skin. Everything had gone without a hitch. I thought about Laura and myself and our life together in the exclusive Mentone Avenue. She had no idea about this, and I would not enlighten her. After a decent interval, I would propose to her, and we would live happily ever after. Life was indeed good. I began to hum.

***

www.ingramcontent.com/pod-product-compliance
Lightning Source LLC
LaVergne TN
LVHW041847070526
838199LV00045BA/1489